Dear Reader,

One of the more enjoyable aspects of my research trip to Los Angeles with my editor was the designing of the apartment building for Bachelor Arms. It is a composite of several wonderful old houses we found in the Melrose and Wilshire Districts. The moment I saw the marvellous Gothic-style turret, I knew I somehow had to fit it into my story.

In this third and final book of the trilogy, both Cait and Lily have now found true love and are engaged to be married. Only Blythe, whose aborted wedding brought everyone together in the first book, *Never a Bride*, has failed to find her happy ending.

Which, of course, she will, with Gage Remington, the sexy private detective she's hired. But first they must outwit a killer determined to keep the sixty-year-old truth of Alexandra Romanov's death buried with the glamorous murdered movie star.

Despite attempts on Blythe's life, and a shocking revelation that shatters their preconceived notions of love and life, by the time they join the others at the altar, Blythe and Gage will have discovered that love is truly better the second time around.

Happy Reading!

JoAnn Ross

BACHELOR ARMS

Come live and love in L.A. with the tenants of Bachelor Arms

Bachelor Arms is a trendy apartment building with some very colourful tenants. Meet three confirmed bachelors who are determined to stay single until three very special women turn their lives upside down; college friends who reunite to plan a wedding; a cynical and sexy lawyer; a director who's renowned for his hedonistic life-style, and many more…including one very mysterious and legendary tenant. And while everyone tries to ignore the legend, every once in a while something strange happens…

Each of these fascinating people has a tale of success or failure, love or heartbreak. But their stories don't stay a secret for long in the hallways of Bachelor Arms.

BACHELOR ARMS

THE TENANTS OF BACHELOR ARMS

Ken Amberson: The odd superintendent who knows more than he admits about the legend of Bachelor Arms.

Connor Mackay: The building's temporary handyman isn't telling the truth about who he really is.

Caitlin Carrigan: For this cop, her career is her priority.

Eddie Cassidy: Local bartender at Flynn's next door. He's looking for his big break as a screenwriter.

Jill Foyle: This sexy, recently divorced interior designer moved to L.A. to begin a new life.

Lily Van Cortlandt: This vulnerable, loving woman can forgive anything other than betrayal.

Natasha Kuryan: This elderly Russian-born femme fatale was a make-up artist to the stars of yesterday.

Gage Remington: Cait Carrigan's former partner is investigating a decades-old murder that involves the residents of Bachelor Arms.

Brenda Muir: Young, enthusiastic would-be actress who supports herself as a waitress.

Bobbie-Sue O'Hara: Brenda's best friend. She works as an actress and waitress but knows that real power lies on the other side of the camera.

Bob Robinson: This barfly seems to live at Flynn's and has an opinion about everyone and everything.

Theodore "Teddy" Smith: The resident Lothario—any new female in the building puts a sparkle in his eye.

THREE GROOMS AND A WEDDING

BY

JoANN ROSS

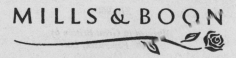

MILLS & BOON

All the characters in this book have no existence outside the imagination
of the author, and have no relation whatsoever to anyone bearing the
same name or names. They are not even distantly inspired by any
individual known or unknown to the author, and all the incidents are
pure invention.

MILLS & BOON and the Rose Device are trademarks of the publisher.
TEMPTATION is a trademark of Harlequin Enterprises II B.V., used
under licence.
First published in Great Britain 1996
by Harlequin Mills & Boon Limited, Eton House, 18-24 Paradise Road,
Richmond, Surrey TW9 1SR

ISBN 0 263 79766 X

21 - 9604

Printed in Great Britain by
BPC Paperbacks Ltd

Prologue

IT WAS AFTER MIDNIGHT. A new day. A new year. A ghostly white moon rode high in the sky, creating a silver glow over the City of Angels.

The hour of celebration had passed. The sounds of "Auld Lang Syne" had given way to the soft rustle of the breeze in the tops of the palm trees. Most of Los Angeles was sleeping, blissfully unaware that one of Hollywood's most infamous murders was about to take place.

Alexandra Romanov Reardon paced the marble floors of her pink Spanish-style mansion, anxiety radiating from every fragrant pore. A passionate woman by nature, with each long stride her mood swung from furious, to desperate, to anxious, then back to furious.

Where was he? How dare he treat her this way! How dare he humiliate her in front of everyone! Didn't he know who she was?

Of course he did.

And that, Alexandra thought wretchedly, was the problem.

She heard a car cruise by outside on the silent street. Thinking—praying!—it might be him, she flung open the door and ran down the sidewalk, prepared to throw her arms around her husband, to smother that dark, handsome face with kisses, and, if necessary, plead for forgiveness.

Alexandra had never begged to any man.

With Patrick she feared begging was inevitable. Just as their marriage had been inevitable.

She'd fallen head over heels in love with the tough-talking writer the moment she'd first seen him, across the crowded room at Xanadu Studios' annual Christmas party.

Less than twenty minutes after meeting, they were making love in the back seat of a cloud white Rolls-Royce convertible.

A week later, on New Year's Day, Xanadu Studios' ultraglamorous sex goddess had become Mrs. Patrick Reardon.

Hollywood pundits had given the marriage a month. Defying the odds, Alexandra and Patrick proved them wrong. Today was their first anniversary, and although they were currently experiencing a few problems—all right, Alexandra admitted reluctantly as she watched the taillights of the unfamiliar yellow Packard turn the corner and disappear from sight, a great many problems—she refused to believe that they couldn't work things out.

Russian enough to believe in fate, Alexandra had known from that first stunning moment of shared recognition, that she and Patrick were destined to be together. For all time. They were soul mates, their love so strong, so everlasting, that nothing—or no one—could ever separate them.

"So where is he?" Alexandra agonized.

It had grown cold. Smoke from the smudge pots that nearby orange growers burned during these winter nights to warm their groves wafted on the salt air. Barely clad in the dangerously low-cut, clinging white satin gown she'd worn to last night's party, she began to shiver.

Returning inside, Alexandra went into the dressing room adjoining the master bedroom suite and retrieved an ivory negligee from her walk-in closet. She'd purchased the exquisite piece of lingerie especially for tonight and having no doubt that once her husband's temper cooled, he'd return, she wanted to be ready for the passionate lovemaking that always followed one of their arguments.

She stepped out of her evening dress, leaving it on the floor in a pool of shimmering satin. Standing in front of the full-length mirror, as she did each morning and every night without fail, Alexandra studied her nude body with an unflinching, critical eye.

Understanding that her popularity among moviegoers was based more on her looks than any innate acting ability, she exercised relentlessly, was rigid about her diet, and avoided the harsh California sun with such diligence friends had laughingly accused her of being part vampire.

"Walter is not going to be at all happy about this," she said with a resigned sigh. That was the understatement of the decade. Frowning as she envisioned the studio executive's explosive reaction when she told him her news, Alexandra turned sideways, running her palms over the voluptuous curves that raised temperatures in movie theaters all over America.

Studying her body as an engineer might study a piece of steel he intended to use as a bridge span, she noted that her breasts were visibly fuller, and her nipples appeared darker, more the color of a rich Bordeaux than their usual raspberry hue. Her stomach was still flat. She pressed her fingertips against the flesh beneath her navel, pleased by the firm muscles she encountered. Splaying her fingers at her waist, she realized that it was already beginning, albeit imperceptibly to a less critical eye, to thicken.

Under normal conditions, this minuscule imperfection would send her into a frenzied flurry of leg lifts and waist twists. But realizing that the change in her body was her baby making its presence known changed everything.

Although she never would have believed it possible, Alexandra was actually looking forward to becoming ripe and round with Patrick's child.

How much had changed in one short year, she thought with a slow smile that overrode her earlier frown. How much she had changed!

When she'd met Patrick she'd been the most envied woman in the world. And the unhappiest.

Now, despite tonight's heated altercation, Alexandra felt herself to be the luckiest. It would not be easy; she understood that it would take Patrick time to accept her admittedly less than pristine past.

But she also knew that he loved her with a passion so deep that sometimes it almost frightened her. He wouldn't be able to stay away.

"Especially when he learns about you," she murmured. Pressing her palms against her stomach, Alexandra imagined her child stirring at his mother's touch.

She slipped the nightgown over her head. The ivory lace was so delicate it appeared to have been created from cobwebs. Beneath it, her perfumed and powdered flesh gleamed like alabaster.

She did not exactly look like a mother-to-be, Alexandra decided. Actually, she looked like the woman who'd recently been blasted in the Congressional Record by a Southern senator who'd called the waterfall scene in her latest film—*Lady Reckless*—dangerous for young male minds and an affront against American decency.

She heard the front door open.

Every nerve ending in her body was thrumming with anticipation. She fluffed up her thick sable hair with her hands, licked her lips and turned to greet her husband.

"I'm in here, Patrick." Her throaty voice offered not contrition, but seduction.

When she was greeted by silence, a frisson of fear skipped up her spine. The day she and Patrick had moved into their new home shortly after their marriage, their neighbor, a contract writer at United Artists, had warned them that the house, which had been the scene of a mysterious death, was haunted.

Live in it and your greatest wish could be granted. Or your greatest fear realized.

Alexandra had worried; her pragmatic western husband had laughed the story off, declaring it the product of the melodramatic screenwriter's warped imagination.

"Patrick?" This time her voice held an uncharacteristic tremor. She wiped her damp palms on her lace negligee.

As the door to the dressing room slowly opened, Alexandra felt a cooling wave of relief.

"You scared me to death!" she said on a shaky laugh.

The morning dawned bright and inappropriately golden. The day before the premiere of her new movie, *Fool's Gold,* based on Patrick's screenplay, on what should have been her first wedding anniversary, Alexandra was found dead in the dressing room of the mansion she shared with her husband.

The coroner ruled she'd been strangled.

1

IT WAS HER OWN SCREAM that woke her.

Blythe Fielding was bathed in a cold sweat. Gasping, struggling desperately for breath, she could taste the salty tears streaming down her face. The nightmare had come just before dawn, creeping into her subconscious like a black cat on All Hallows' Eve.

She should be used to them by now, Blythe thought grimly as she struggled to extricate herself from the damp and tangled sheets. But how could one get accustomed to nightly terror? After suffering the threatening images for weeks this one had been the worst so far.

She reached out a trembling hand, managing to turn on the bedside lamp on the second try. She'd discovered the night demons lost their powers when a bright light was turned on them.

Momentarily blinded by the sudden glare, she closed her eyes and took several deep breaths, willing herself to calm. They couldn't hurt her, she reminded herself. Not really. They were only dreams.

So why did it all seem so horribly real?

The air conditioner was on, sending cool air blowing over her moist skin. Shivering, Blythe climbed out of bed, stripped off her soaked nightshirt and exchanged it for a fresh, dry one.

She went around the bedroom, turning on every lamp, including the lights in the adjoining bathroom. Standing in front of the full-length mirror, she lifted a hand to her throat, absently rubbing the unmarked flesh that strangely, inexplicably felt as if it were burning.

Feeling foolish, but unable to help herself, she went into the living room and turned on all the lights in there, as well.

With the hotel bungalow now ablaze in brightness, she sat bolt upright in a flowered wing chair and waited for morning.

"YOU LOOK LIKE HELL."

Cait Carrigan frowned as she studied her longtime friend over the umbrella-topped breakfast table. Film buffs might recognize the Sunset Boulevard restaurant as the one where Woody Allen made New York-centric disparaging remarks about southern California in the movie, *Annie Hall*.

"Gee, thanks." Blythe picked dispiritedly at her vegetarian omelet. "It's always nice to know I can count on my friends for flattery."

The two friends, one reminiscent of a bright flame, the other as sultry as a Gypsy, created an attractive foil for one another. More than one passing male slowed to admire them, but accustomed to appreciative glances from the opposite sex, neither Cait nor Blythe noticed.

"This town is overflowing with false flattery. What you need is someone to tell you the truth." Concern shadowed Cait's expressive green eyes. "Are you still having problems with your Alexandra Romanov project?"

To her international legion of fans, Blythe Fielding was a superstar. To Cait, she was a lifelong friend.

Having recently formed her own production company, parlaying her box office fame into a multipicture deal with Xanadu Studios, Blythe was determined that her company's first film tell the story of star-crossed lovers, Alexandra Romanov and Patrick Reardon.

The brutal death of the glamorous, tempestuous 1930s sex symbol at the hands of her hot-tempered husband, who'd subsequently been executed for his crime, had been the scandal of the decade.

"Since everything about the project has turned out to be a problem, I'd be surprised if anything did go right," Blythe answered.

"So it's not responsible for the shadows beneath your eyes?"

Blythe sighed and absently lifted her fingers to the purple smudges. "I think everything is beginning to pile up on me," she admitted. "I've finally gotten the insurance settlement for the house, but every time I turn around, the contractor has disappeared."

"He's probably juggling jobs," Cait suggested as she spread a thick layer of orange marmalade onto an oversize date muffin. "It's only been about three months since the earthquake. There's a lot of reconstruction work out there to do."

"I know." Another sigh. "It's just that I'm getting tired of living in a hotel."

"You could always move in with Alan."

Alan Sturgess was Blythe's fiancé. The earthquake that had caused her lovely Beverly Hills home to be condemned had also resulted in disrupting her garden wedding to the famed plastic surgeon to the stars.

"The subject has come up," Blythe admitted.

Cait arched a red-gold brow and eyed her friend over the rim of her coffee cup. "Do I hear a 'but' in that statement?"

"I don't know."

Blythe shook her head and wondered what had gotten into her lately. It hadn't been that long ago that she'd thought she'd had her life completely planned.

Since her deal with Walter Stern at Xanadu Studios required her to make two movies of his choosing for every one her production company made, she'd grown resigned to the oversexed, underdressed roles.

As much as she hated being typecast, she'd been willing to do it, in order to win the power to produce. But then the studio had been sold to Connor Mackay, who coincidentally was now engaged to Blythe's other close friend, Lily Van Cortlandt, and Walter Stern appeared to be on his way out.

And although Connor had assured her of his support for her pet project, Blythe continued to have misgivings about ever bringing the film to the screen.

In addition to the problems with her home, and at work, Alan had been pushing her to set a new date for their wedding. And heaven help her, something was holding her back.

"It's not that I'm not fond of Alan, because I am—"

"Fond?" Cait jumped on the term like a sleek lioness might spring onto an unsuspecting springbok. "Isn't that a bit mild for a man you're about to promise to spend the rest of your life with?"

The morning sun slipped beneath the umbrella. Partly to shade her eyes from the bright rays and partly to shield them from Cait's intense scrutiny, Blythe slipped on her sunglasses.

"It's complicated," she murmured, pretending a sudden interest in the morning traffic streaming down Sunset.

"Love is always complicated," Cait said with the air of a woman who'd recently experienced her own romantic entanglements. "But, in the end it's worth the trouble."

Watching the soft color drift into her friend's cheeks at the thought of the man who'd finally managed to breach the daunting parapets surrounding Cait Carrigan's heart, Blythe felt a faint tinge of envy.

"That's what Lily was telling me last night," she admitted.

"Lord knows, Lily should be an expert by now," Cait said. "When she was trapped in that horrid marriage, she probably never imagined meeting a man who adored her—and her baby—like Connor does."

"He does dote on them." The memory of the sexy multimillionaire inexpertly changing a pink polka-dot diaper made her smile. "After all Lily's been through, she deserves to be happy."

"Amen." Cait lifted her glass of orange juice in a toast of agreement. "You know," she said, carefully testing the waters, "Connor isn't the only man who thinks Lily walks on water. You should hear the way Gage talks about her."

Gage Remington was Cait's former partner and the private detective Blythe had hired to dig up information on Alexandra's life. And although she'd tried to deny it, even to herself, he was also the man responsible for her ambivalence toward her fiancé.

From the first moment they'd met, on the deck of the sloop he used as an office—before it sank in the earthquake—she'd experienced a shock of recognition so strong, it was as if she'd been struck by a bolt of lightning.

"I know Gage thinks Lily's invaluable," Blythe agreed blandly, sidestepping Cait's artful probe regarding her relationship with the detective. "And I think it's marvelous that they've gone into partnership together."

"Our Lily, a P. I." Cait laughed. "Who would have ever guessed?" Cait was nothing if not tenacious. She leaned back in her chair, crossed her legs, gave Blythe a long look and said, "Gage told me you two are going to Greece together."

"That's right. Tomorrow morning. We're trying to track down Natasha."

Natasha Kuryan had been Alexandra's former makeup artist at Xanadu. A resident of Cait's apartment building, Bachelor Arms, Natasha had jumped ship during a recent tour of the Greek Islands and had reportedly become romantically involved with a local author of her own generation. That she had to be in her eighties did not seem to have slowed down Natasha's love life.

In her four years on the L.A. police force, Cait had come to read faces well. Watching the storm of emotions move across Blythe's face, she suspected she knew the cause of much of her best friend's uncharacteristic behavior.

"You're falling in love with him, aren't you?"

"Alan?" Blythe asked with feigned innocence. She was not an actress for nothing.

"Don't try to blow me off, kiddo," Cait warned. "In the first place, I'm a dynamite interrogator, so you don't stand a chance. In the second place, I've known you forever. I'm talking about Gage."

Blythe shook her head. "It would be a horrendous mistake."

She did not, Cait noticed, answer the question. "Why?" Close to both Gage and Blythe, Cait found the match ideal.

Blythe sighed. How could she explain that her emotions toward Gage were confusing and complex? How could she make Cait understand that her feelings were, at the same time, both familiar and foreign? "I'm engaged," she hedged, choosing her words with care.

"Engagements can be broken." And if she'd ever seen one that should be, Cait considered, Blythe's engagement to the stuffy, self-important surgeon was it.

"It would create a scandal."

"Probably." Blythe was, after all, a star. The breakup would garner even more tabloid attention than when Julia Roberts had called off her fairy-tale wedding. "But it'd blow over. It always does."

Since Cait's own parents had set the Hollywood record for matrimonial musical beds, Blythe knew the remark came from firsthand experience. Experience that had once had Cait swearing off men altogether. Until she met Sloan Wyndham, a stubborn, independent, extremely talented screenwriter who refused to take no for an answer.

"The problem is, in the meantime, until the tabloids find some other victim to smear all over their front pages, I could ruin Alan's chances for becoming chief of staff."

"I don't believe this!" Cait's bright brows drew together. "Are you saying you're willing to marry a man you don't love, just to keep from damaging his chances for career advancement?"

Blythe looked away again. "When you put it like that, I suppose it does sound a little silly."

"How about downright ridiculous?" She reached across the table and grasped Blythe's hand. "I'm sure Alan is a brilliant surgeon. He's also undoubtedly honest and dependable and as solid as the Rock of Gibraltar. But he's not the man for you, Blythe."

Cait had been saying that from the beginning. And from the beginning Blythe had been refusing to listen.

Blythe looked down at their joined hands and stifled a weary sigh. She was so tired. So confused.

"I told you," she insisted quietly, "my reasons for marrying Alan go beyond some fleeting passion that won't last past the first anniversary."

"Yeah, yeah, I know." Cait waved her words away with an impatient left hand. An emerald as bright as her eyes and surrounded by diamonds splintered the morning light. "Alan Sturgess will make a good father to your children and he's not in the movie business." She'd heard it innumerable times before. And she still wasn't buying it.

"That's important," Blythe insisted. She retrieved her hand and dragged it through her thick sable hair. A lifetime of Hollywood experience had taught her that most actors tended to be too egocentric and immature to make long-term marriages.

"You know *I* swore never to get involved with anyone in the business," Cait reminded her. "Until I fell in love with the man who's currently spending nearly every waking minute writing your screenplay."

In spite of the all too familiar argument regarding her fiancé, Blythe smiled. "Sloan's special."

"You can say that again." Cait sat back in her chair once more and enjoyed the flow of warmth that thinking about Sloan Wyndham could bring. "Do you believe in love at first sight?"

"Not really," Blythe answered. What she and Gage had experienced was a long way from love. Lust. Desire. Hunger. Even need. Unfortunately, knowing the jolt of emotion that had forked through her wasn't really love, hadn't made it any less potent.

"I never did, either." Cait's eyes took on a faraway, misty look Blythe envied. "But you know, I think I fell in love with Sloan from the moment I saw him."

"If memory serves, the moment you saw him, you pulled a 9 mm Glock, told him to freeze, then handcuffed him to my driveway gate."

Cait shrugged. Her grin was wide and unabashed. "So I thought I was falling in love with a burglar. It happens."

"In the movies," Blythe argued mildly.

"Sometimes, if you're lucky, real life is even better than the movies." Cait's smile faded, her expression sobered. "You know, Gage is special, too."

"I know." Blythe's voice was so atypically faint, so uncharacteristically unsure, Cait felt a surge of sympathy.

"Let me say just one last thing," she said, "and I promise, I'll drop the subject for today."

Her relief evident, Blythe nodded her assent.

Cait's warm candid gaze settled on Blythe's face as she reached across the table again and gave her friend's hand a quick, reassuring squeeze.

"You can run, Blythe. But only so far. And so long."

And that, Blythe thought miserably, was exactly what she was afraid of. As she left the restaurant, she couldn't shake off the feeling that her life was about to change. In ways she couldn't even begin to imagine.

Although she'd grown up in the business, Blythe experienced a rush of excitement each time she drove through the ornate, wrought iron gates of Xanadu Studios. It was, in the truest sense of the words, a Dream Factory. For seventy-five years the studio had been supplying an eager audience with fantasy. And although she, more than most, understood that moviemaking was actually a business, complete with corporate concerns, internal power struggles and bottom-line budgetary requirements, there would always be a vast difference between selling dreams and selling soap.

She'd come here today for a meeting with Walter Stern III, grandson of the studio founder and current president. Although, she mused, as she walked down the hallway lined with photos of the studio's stars and cases displaying the studio's myriad Oscars, now that Connor Mackay was the new owner and CEO of Xanadu, Walter's position was more than a little tenuous.

Having known the studio executive all her life, Blythe was well aware that he was not a man accustomed to sharing power. As for taking orders . . .

She shook her head, unable to imagine Connor and Walter working together.

His secretary, who'd guarded access to Stern's inner sanctum for the past twenty-five years, greeted Blythe warmly. "He said to send you right in," Margaret Nelson said. Although her smile was as friendly as ever, Blythe viewed the worry in the woman's gray eyes.

"Thanks." She paused. "How's the takeover going?"

"As well as can be expected." Margaret sighed and dragged her hand through her graying auburn hair. "Mr. Mackay seems terribly nice. But it's obvious that he intends to take a hands-on approach to running the studio and . . ." She glanced at the thick rosewood door leading into her boss's office and shrugged.

"I know," Blythe commiserated. Although she did not feel any loyalty toward Stern, who'd made her life difficult on more than one occasion, she hated seeing a woman with Margaret's talent and tenure laid off through no fault of her own. "I can't see a partnership working out, either."

They shared a grim look. Then, wishing the secretary luck, Blythe opened the office door.

"Blythe." Walter's wide smile did not reveal a scintilla of trouble. He rose from behind his enormous Chinese lacquered desk to greet her. "Thank you for coming in."

As she felt herself being enfolded in his arms, Blythe had to fight against stiffening in response. When he appeared prepared to hold her just a bit too long for a casual hug, she pressed her hands against his shoulders and extricated herself.

"It's no problem," she lied. The meeting, called at the last minute yesterday, was a definite inconvenience.

"Can I have Margaret get you anything? Tea? Coffee? Pelligrino?"

"Actually, I wasn't planning to stay that long, Walter. I still have a great many last minute things to get out of the way today."

"Before your trip to Greece." His expression was smooth as glass, but she thought she detected a hint of tension in his voice.

"Yes." She sat down in one of the suede chairs on the visitor's side of the desk. The desk itself, and the executive chair behind it, was on a three-inch high platform, requiring anyone doing business with Stern to look up at him.

"Do you really have time for this trip?" he asked solicitously. "What with your own project and *Expose* to begin shooting this winter?"

Expose was yet one more of the movies she'd agreed to do for Xanadu in order to get the studio's cooperation in releasing films made by her fledgling production company. Although the story was in its eighth—or ninth, she couldn't keep track—rewrite, the last script she'd seen had something to do with a high-priced call girl entering into a partnership with a reporter to expose political corruption that went all the way to the presidency.

She would, of course, play the call girl, and although Tom Cruise had originally been mentioned for the part of the reporter, the latest word was that Stern was negotiating with Keanu Reeves, who was currently the hottest property in town.

The film would not, Blythe knew, earn her an Oscar nomination. But it would make a great deal of money. And most importantly, it would allow her to make movies she could be proud of.

"The timing's going to be tight," she admitted. "But I need to talk to Natasha Kuryan. And since she's currently in Greece, I don't have any choice but to go there."

"Natasha Kuryan." He leaned back, braced his elbows on the arms of his chair and made a tent of his fingers. "I can't believe the woman's still alive."

"Very much so, if the stories can be believed," Blythe said dryly, thinking about what Gage had told her about Natasha's current romantic relationship with a Greek author. "Did you know her?"

"No." He shook his head. "She was, of course, before my time. She was gone before I began working here, but I do remember my grandfather mentioning her. He called her the Rembrandt of the makeup artists."

"Or the Mary Cassatt." At his blank look, she elaborated, "Since Natasha's a woman, it probably makes more sense to compare her to a woman artist."

"There you go, getting politically correct on me again," he said with a flash of bonded teeth. "Honestly, Blythe, if you don't tone down your feminist rhetoric, you'll end up losing your audience."

"Speaking her mind certainly hasn't seemed to hurt Susan Sarandon's box office appeal," Blythe returned mildly.

"Touché," he said with what she recognized as false cheer.

Blythe didn't have time to rehash old arguments. "Is there some special reason you called me here today, Walter?" She cast a significant glance at her watch. "Because I really am pressed for time."

"That's precisely my point." He leaned forward and looked down at her. His jaw was set in a way that reminded her of a bulldog. "I want to warn you about Natasha."

"Warn me?"

"Although I understand how frustrating it's been for you, trying to get your first project off the ground, you're making a mistake thinking that Natasha Kuryan can help you."

"She knew Alexandra intimately," Blythe argued. "She also knew Patrick."

Blythe had even heard rumors that the writer and the makeup artist had an adulterous fling. Believing that whatever their problems, there had never been any other woman for Patrick Reardon besides Alexandra, after their first meeting at that Xanadu Christmas party, Blythe had discounted the stories.

"That may be. But her memory is not to be trusted."

Blythe arched an argumentative brow. She never seemed to be able to have a conversation with this man without getting into an argument. "Just because she's elderly?"

"No. Because she's a liar. Or crazy." Brackets formed on either side of his mouth; his scowl created deep furrows in his tanned forehead. "Hell, probably both." He leaned back again and seemed to be struggling to relax. "My father had to fire her, you know."

"Oh?"

"She was telling dangerous lies about things that had happened at the studio. Things about my grandfather."

"I didn't know anything about that." Blythe felt the tension in the room, like the threat of a thunderstorm on the horizon.

"Well, now you do." His expression cleared. "Of course you're free to do whatever you wish, Blythe. I just didn't want you to be disappointed."

"Thank you, Walter." Annoyed that she'd driven all the way to the Valley just to hear something he could have told her over the phone, something she was not going to allow to stop her from tracking Natasha Kuryan down, Blythe rose from her chair. "I appreciate your concern."

He stood up as well. And this time he was forestalled from hugging her by her outstretched hand.

"I know we've crossed swords from time to time, Blythe." His fingers clasped hers with a force that almost made her flinch. "But I've always had your best interests at heart."

"I appreciate that as well." He wasn't the only one who could lie. "Goodbye, Walter. I'll call you when I get back."

"I'll be looking forward to it." He released her hand and, as he walked her to the door, placed his palm lightly, possessively, on her hip. "Perhaps you can tell me all about your adventures over dinner. I have a new cook who does wonders with swordfish."

A seductive note had crept into his voice. One Blythe had heard too many times before. They'd be having snowball fights on Rodeo Drive before she allowed herself to be alone with this man at his Bel Air mansion. Stories of his sexual conquests—some not entirely consensual—were common knowledge in Hollywood. Blythe knew it continued to irritate him that she refused to allow herself to become just another notch on the man's headboard.

She was on her way back down the hallway when a familiar voice called out her name. Turning, she grinned at Lily's new fiancé.

This man's hug she welcomed. "Hello, Connor." She hugged him back.

"What are you doing here?" he asked. "I thought you and Gage were on your way to Greece."

"Tomorrow." Blythe knew she was in trouble the way even hearing Gage Remington's name could make her heart skip a beat. "I dropped by because Walter wanted to see me."

"Oh?" Although his smile didn't fade, Blythe, who was watching him carefully, did not miss the way his dark eyes suddenly shuttered. "May I ask what he wanted?"

"He tried to talk me out of going to Greece to meet with Natasha Kuryan about Alexandra and Patrick."

"Do you have a minute?" he asked suddenly.

She didn't. Not really. But for this man who'd brought so much joy into Lily's life, Blythe would make time. "Sure."

"Let's go into my office."

Unlike Walter Stern's status office, Connor's was as comfortable and accessible as the man himself. The furniture, while expensive, had been built for comfort, not to impress. Antique movie posters, some she knew to be almost priceless, adorned white walls.

Rather than take the power position behind his rosewood desk, Connor led her to the couch, then sat in a facing suede chair. "There's something you should know," he said. "But I'm going to ask you to keep it to yourself until Friday."

"Of course." Blythe had a feeling she knew what was coming.

"Walter's on his way out."

"I'm not surprised," she murmured. "May I ask why?"

"Several reasons." He leaned forward and linked his fingers between his knees. His expression sobered. "In the first place, since he's the one who ran the company into near bankruptcy, I don't have a great deal of confidence in his financial abilities."

"All Xanadu's films make money," Blythe felt obliged to point out.

"True. But most of it goes for things like those Jackson Pollock paintings in his office and the remodeling of his place in Aspen."

"It was a family studio."

"The definitive word there is *was*." His dark eyes turned so dark as to be almost black. His chiseled jaw hardened. "The guy can't seem to get it through his head that Xanadu is no longer his personal piggy bank."

When she'd first met Connor Mackay, he'd been masquerading as the temporary handyman at Bachelor Arms. At the time, she'd thought that there was something about the man that didn't quite fit his alleged profession. Now, looking at the intelligence, and the determination in those dark eyes, Blythe could easily see him as the multimillionaire wheeler-dealer he'd turned out to be.

"You said that was one of the reasons."

"Another is the studio's choice of subject matter. I'll be the first to admit that films like *Expose*, *Night Stalker*, and *Bomb Squad* make money. But there's plenty of

room to make other films as well. Films with social con-
science. Or, strong, character-driven stories like the one
you and Sloan are working on."

Blythe relaxed. She'd been so worried that Connor
might not continue to support her project. "You've no
idea what a load that is off my mind," she admitted.

He looked surprised. "I told you I liked the idea,
Blythe."

"True. But I thought perhaps, because of Lily—"

"That I would compromise my beliefs?" he inter-
rupted. "No. I love Lily to distraction. But if I'd been reluctant to continue with your Alexandra project, Blythe,
I would have told you straight out." He flashed her the
quick, warm smile that Lily had, against her will, found
unable to resist.

"I'll admit that the way we met doesn't say much for
my credibility, but I've always prided myself on being
straightforward."

Understanding the tangled web of lies he'd inadver-
tently gotten himself into in an attempt to win over a ro-
mance-shy Lily, Blythe returned his smile with a warm
one of her own.

"I know. Cait and I were saying just this morning how
lucky Lily is to have you."

"I'm the lucky one." The smile warmed his eyes. "To
have Lily. And Kate." Blythe knew that Connor had been
the one to insist on naming the baby after Lily's mother.

"There's another reason Stern has to go," Connor revealed. "Have you met Brenda Muir?"

"The would-be actress living at Bachelor Arms? Bub-
bly, naive and gorgeous?"

"That's her. She recently had an audition with Walter."

"Ah." Blythe nodded. "And Walter, being Walter, couldn't resist trying to get her onto his casting couch."

"You don't sound surprised."

Blythe shrugged. "I was fifteen years old when he first tried that on me. He showed up on the set one day, visited me in my trailer and tried to rip off my blouse."

Anger stirred. Connor quenched it, reminding himself that the guy was on his way out. Having always looked toward the future, it was not in his nature to dwell on the past.

"What did you do?" He hoped this would not be some tawdry tale of teenage rape. Because then he would not only have to fire Stern, but punch him out for hurting his wife's best friend.

"I gave him a black eye. Then told my father, who threatened to file charges." A much admired entertainment attorney, David Fielding was one of the few people in town who possessed clout equal to that of the studio owner. "Dad also, as a side note, threatened to kill him if he ever laid a hand on me again. I don't know if Walter was more afraid of the scandal or death, but he pretty much left me alone after that."

"I'm glad to hear that. Unfortunately, not every young woman is as gutsy as you, and Brenda fortunately turned out to be."

"Some *are* more desperate. And unfortunately, although it's not talked about out in the open anymore, sleeping your way to the top didn't end with the studio system."

"True. But it's not going to be the way business is conducted at Xanadu. Not anymore."

"You've just made the female employees, not to mention half the actresses in town, extremely happy." That brought up another question. "What about Margaret?"

she asked, concerned for the ultraefficient secretary's future.

"I'd planned to ask her if she'd consider becoming my personal assistant."

"That's very thoughtful of you."

"It's the logical thing to do," he said, shrugging off her compliment. "I need someone familiar with the day-to-day business of running Xanadu. And hiring Margaret Nelson appears to be one of the few good judgments Stern's made during his tenure here."

"It's still a nice thing to do." Once again, Blythe thought how fortunate Lily was to have found this man. How fortunate they were to have found each other.

"Well, I didn't mean to keep you." Connor stood up. "I just wanted to fill you in, since you're going to be out of the country when Stern's shown the door."

"With a golden parachute," she guessed.

"Movies may tend to put things in nice, neat little boxes, where the good guys are rewarded in the last reel and the bad guys run out of town on a rail.

"Unfortunately, life is messier than cinema. Stern will be leaving with a generous buyout. But at least he'll be gone. And that's the important thing."

Connor had made the only decision possible, Blythe thought as she drove back through those elaborate gates personally designed by the first Stern to run Xanadu. Still, even knowing Connor Mackay's brilliant business reputation, she feared that getting rid of Walter Stern III would be easier said than done.

Like his father, and his grandfather before him, the man was infamous for fighting dirty when something he wanted was at stake. She had an ominous feeling that her friend's husband-to-be was in for the battle of his life.

2

A STORM WAS BREWING. Dark clouds were building up on the horizon, the air had turned electric. Telling himself that the painful needles beneath his skin had everything to do with the weather, and nothing to do with the fact that tomorrow morning he was leaving for Greece with a woman he could not get out of his mind, Gage Remington dragged a duffel bag from beneath the bed and began throwing underwear into it.

He'd always prided himself on his control. During his days on the force, patrolling the gang neighborhoods of South Central L.A., he'd developed a reputation for being tough, fair and unflappable.

It hadn't taken long for the word to get out: if you were looking for a cop to defuse a dangerous situation, Gage Remington was your man. Control had been his watchword; patience his forte.

Unfortunately, when it came to Blythe Fielding, control and patience were proving to be in scant supply.

Not since his testosterone-driven teenage days had he felt so damn horny. He went to bed each night with his groin aching and woke up each morning hot and hard. And unfulfilled.

"Damn her!"

He dragged his hand through his black hair and cursed. He had a job to do. She was only an employer. And even if the lady had him burning from the inside out, to get involved with her would be madness.

If it was merely physical, he could handle it. From that first moment they had met on his boat, the chemistry had been instantaneous and undeniable. And if that kiss he'd stolen the day after the earthquake was any indication, the sex between them would be incomparable.

Having experienced the seamy underbelly beneath the city's glitter, Gage knew, better than most, that Hollywood was a place of images and illusions. But, if her uncontrolled response to him that afternoon was any indication, amazingly, Blythe was even more passionate than the sultry femme fatale roles she invariably played up on that oversize screen.

Just as he hadn't been able to get their steamy kiss from his mind, neither had Gage been able to forget the way she'd felt beneath him when they'd been knocked to the ground by the earthquake's first massive jolt.

Beneath the ivory satin wedding dress, her body had been lush and fragrant; her voluptuous curves had fit against his body so perfectly she could have been designed with him in mind. Ever since that day, as hard as he fought against it, the seductive thought of being surrounded by that hot feminine flesh had kept him in a constant state of near arousal.

The problem plaguing both his waking and sleeping mind was that Gage feared that a great deal more was involved here than chemistry.

Blythe Fielding was the kind of woman who could not only get under a man's skin, but infiltrate his mind, and even worse, his heart. And for a man who'd always managed to avoid emotional entanglement, Gage was finding that idea even more dangerous than anything he'd ever faced during his days on the force.

"She's just a woman," he muttered, the same damn thing he'd been telling himself for weeks. "A gorgeous, sexy woman, granted. But this town is overflowing with gorgeous, sexy females."

So why did Blythe Fielding have his insides all tied up in knots?

The first time Blythe visited Cait at Bachelor Arms, she'd experienced a sudden, unbidden feeling of déjà vu. As impossible as it seemed, each subsequent time she pulled up in front of the Mediterranean pink house, with its turquoise trim, lacy iron grillwork, balconies and odd turret, rather than diminishing, the strangely familiar feeling intensified.

And if she'd felt uneasy visiting Cait, as she headed down the hallway and approached Gage Remington's apartment door, Blythe was strangely torn between walking right in without knocking and running away.

She really was in trouble, she considered as she rapped at the door. When even the man's apartment made her feel so uncharacteristically ambivalent.

A sound at the door broke Gage's frustrated thoughts.

Hell. As if conjured up by his mutinous mind, the object of all his consternation—and desire—was standing in his doorway. She was wearing a red silk blouse and a pair of taupe linen slacks, but she would have been no more alluring had she been draped in Salome's diaphanous veils. Even as simply dressed as she was, she still managed to exude pure, undiluted sex. Looking down at her, Gage discovered, all too painfully, that hunger had claws.

"This is a surprise." Tamping down the pleasure, he concentrated on control.

"Hi." Her voice was more breathless than it should have been. Her nerves more tangled. "I hate people who drop in without calling, but I was in the neighborhood, and, well, I remembered something I wanted to discuss with you before our flight tomorrow." She took a breath that was meant to calm, but didn't. "So, I took a chance you might be in."

She wasn't fooling either of them. Gage knew that whatever Blythe wanted to talk about could have been handled over the phone. But, encouraged by the fact that she was no more able to stay away from him than he was able to stop thinking about her, he opened the door wide.

"Come on in." Even with his rigid self-control, Blythe could literally feel the energy humming from every pore. A force that was echoed deep inside her. "I hope I'm not interrupting anything."

"I was just packing."

"Oh." She glanced around the apartment with idle curiosity, remembering when she'd first visited it with Cait. It had been vacant then. When her gaze settled on the oversize mirror that literally dominated the room, she tensed. A frisson of something that could have been expectation or fear skimmed up her spine.

"I'd forgotten about this." As if drawn by an extra-powerful magnet she crossed the room and stood in front of the silver-backed glass.

"Sounds as if you've seen it before."

"Cait showed it to me." Unable to resist, Blythe ran her fingers over the pewter frame, tracing the elaborate scrollwork.

Although she told herself that it was only her nerves, stimulated as they always were in Gage's presence, she could have sworn she felt the metal roses warm beneath her touch. "Did anyone tell you about the legend?"

"Jill seems to have left that out."

Gage's tone was thick with disbelief. He hadn't liked the mirror, which was the focal point of the apartment, the first time he'd seen it. These past weeks living with it hadn't changed his mind. If he could have taken it off the wall, he would have. But for some strange reason, the damn thing wouldn't budge. Not wanting to ruin the plaster wall, he'd learned to almost ignore it.

"According to Cait, some people have seen a woman in it."

"Sounds like some people were smoking stuff you can't get from any vending machine."

"Perhaps." Blythe decided not to reveal that both Cait and Connor had seen the mysterious vision. Such stories were their own to tell. "It gets even stranger."

Gage came up behind her. Her scent, a dark, mysterious fragrance that suited her perfectly, filled his senses like a drug and threatened to cloud his mind.

"Why am I not surprised by that?" Personally he figured any alleged legend was something the owner had concocted to give the place some Hollywood pizzazz. Something to go along with the words scratched beneath the plaque on the front wall: *Believe the legend.*

Blythe could feel the warmth emanating from him. It crept into her bones and made her knees weak. Little flickers of flame licked at her stomach, sparked along her skin. Heaven help her, it was happening again! She felt herself on the verge of losing control.

"The legend says if you see the woman in the mirror, your greatest wish could be granted. Or your greatest fear realized."

Tempted to turn around and fling herself into his arms, Blythe resisted looking up at him. Instead, she met his steady, unwavering gaze in the mirror.

Lord, he was incredibly sexy, Blythe thought, not for the first time as she stared at their reflections. Black Irish, with lush jet hair and pale, silvery blue eyes that had a way of looking at her as if they could see all the way to her soul. He was wearing a faded gray police academy T-shirt with a pair of low-riding jeans. His feet were bare and although she told herself that she was losing her mind, even the sight of his long straight toes made her blood swim a little hotter.

The words rang a deep and distant bell. Telling himself that he'd obviously overheard one of the other Bachelor Arms tenants discussing the alleged legend, Gage shrugged the inexplicable memory off.

"Have you seen her?" he asked.

"No." Blythe sternly reminded herself that she was an engaged woman. "But I know people who have."

She was a talented actress. But as hard as she was trying to keep things on an even keel, Gage would have had to have been deaf not to hear the unmasked desire in her voice. He would have had to have been blind not to see the need rise in eyes that were nearly as dark as her hair.

Reigning in his own unruly desire, Gage shrugged. "The power of suggestion can prove surprisingly strong."

"I suppose." She dragged her gaze from the mirror, turned around and forced herself to look up at him.

"The reason I dropped by was to ask if you'd talked to your contact in Greece about Natasha's whereabouts."

As if the elderly woman jumping ship wasn't bad enough, Gage's last report was that her lover had taken her off on a sight-seeing trip of nearby islands.

"Last I heard she was on Seriphos." He'd been right. He could have answered the question over the phone. "But don't worry, we'll find her, wherever she is. It just might take a little more time."

That was exactly what she was afraid of. "How much time?"

"Beats me." Gage idly fantasized keeping Blythe away from Los Angeles—and her stuffed-shirt fiancé—forever. They could lie in the sun, swim in the Mediterranean, feed each other fat succulent grapes, drink ouzo, and dance until dawn in some rustic taverna. And make love, all night long. "I hadn't realized you were pressed for time."

"You knew I'd hoped to get my movie shot before I have to show up on the set for *Exposé*."

"Don't worry, Boss Lady." He skimmed a finger down the slope of her perfectly formed nose. "Remington Investigations is on the case. And we always get our man. Or, in this case, our woman."

Blythe smiled, as she was meant to, and tried to relax.

But later that evening, as she packed for her trip, she realized that as tightly focused as she was in regard to her career, when it came to her personal life, she'd been drifting.

Although she'd begged off having dinner with Alan, claiming the need to finish up some paperwork and pack, Blythe knew she couldn't leave for Greece with Gage without first talking face-to-face with the man who, had it not been for the earthquake hitting during the wedding ceremony, would now be her husband.

Lately, after innumerable conversations with Cait and Lily, Blythe had been forced to take a long hard look at her upcoming marriage. In the beginning, having always prided herself on her commonsense approach to life in a town that seemed to go out of its way to avoid rational behavior, she had considered the handsome, wealthy plastic surgeon a perfect match.

They both had careers that demanded a great deal of time and energy, they were both independent, strong-minded individuals and neither possessed the type of clinging personality that needed constant ego strokes from a spouse. Most importantly, Alan was at the age when a man began to think of establishing a dynasty while Blythe, who'd always wanted a large family, was finding the idea of motherhood increasingly appealing.

Although Hollywood definitely had its share of single parents, Blythe had been surprised to discover that she possessed a deeply traditional streak. Not that she had any intention of staying home and baking chocolate chip cookies while wearing high heels and an apron like Mrs. Cleaver. Having worked all her life, from the time she'd been cast as an Ivory soap baby while still in her cradle, she had no intention of giving up her career.

But, having observed several of her friends struggle to be both mother and father to their children, Blythe had come to the conclusion that when possible, two parents were better than one. Watching Lily and Connor share both the responsibilities and the joys of their new infant daughter had only solidified that belief.

Feeling so strongly about putting marriage before maternity, Blythe now realized that without having realized she'd been doing it, she'd gone looking for a man who would make a good parent.

The problem was, she thought as she rolled down the window on her Jaguar and punched in the code for Alan's electronic driveway gate, she'd been so intent on finding a father figure, she really hadn't given enough consideration to what she wanted in a husband.

Alan was, as she was consistently telling Cait, solid and dependable. And although he did not pretend to either appreciate or understand her work, he had, in his own way, grudgingly come to terms with her career.

As a plastic surgeon, he was intimately familiar with the female body, which made him a good and thorough lover. But he didn't make her blood burn. And he didn't make her bones melt. And though she knew that there was a great deal more to a marriage than sex, she couldn't get a conversation with Lily out of her mind.

It was when her friend had first arrived in Los Angeles, recently widowed, seven months pregnant and coming off a marriage from hell.

Blythe had just revealed her wedding plans, when Lily had asked, "Do you love Alan?"

"Of course," Blythe had answered promptly, ignoring Cait's exaggerated grimace. "I wouldn't be marrying him if I didn't love him."

"And does he love you?"

"Of course."

"Does he make you crazy?"

"If you mean does he have any nagging little flaws—"

"No." Lily's gaze had turned inordinately serious. "I mean, in bed. Does he drive you mad when you make love?"

The question had surprised Blythe. "That's a rather personal question," she'd answered.

But Lily had refused to give up. "You and Cait always told me about the men you slept with," she'd pressed on, seemingly determined to discover the truth. "Why should this be any different?"

"Because Alan's different." Just as she'd hedged when Cait had asked a similar question, Blythe had not been about to admit to those times when she'd felt vaguely disappointed after their lovemaking. "He's the man I love, Lily. The man I'm going to spend the rest of my life with. I don't feel comfortable sharing our intimate moments. Not even with you."

Lily had given her a long, unfathomable look. "I suppose I can understand that. And I realize I don't have all that much experience, but the one thing I have learned, Blythe, is that if a man can't make you fly, and you can't make him burn, you're probably letting yourself in for a lot of pain down the road."

Now, apparently, with Connor, Lily had found a man who could make her fly. And although Blythe was not yet prepared to admit that Gage Remington—or that heated kiss they'd shared—had anything to do with her decision, the reason she'd come to Alan's house this evening was to prove to herself that her upcoming marriage would be one of passion, as well as convenience.

She'd prepared carefully for the occasion. She'd bathed in Shalimar bath oils, had rubbed scented pink cream into every pore, then followed that up with a dusting of matching powder. The strapless teddy she was wearing beneath her short, black form-caressing silk slip dress was as scarlet as sin, designed to light any man's fire. Her stockings were ebony silk, and her shoes boasted four-inch stiletto heels. She'd kept the shoes on impulse after wearing them in her last movie, where she played the adulterous, murderous wife of an FBI agent.

She'd applied her makeup with an artistic flair, exaggerating her dark lips and sultry eyes. Her hair was a wild tousled cloud that made it look as if she'd just left a lover's bed. Looking at her, any man would know at first glance that this was definitely a woman with seduction on her mind.

Not leaving anything to chance, she'd stopped at a liquor store on the way and purchased a bottle of champagne. For the second time today, she was showing up at a man's house unannounced. And although she'd been telling the truth when she'd informed Gage that such behavior was highly uncharacteristic, she was hoping to bring a little—all right, a lot, she admitted—of spontaneity to her relationship with her fiancé.

She rang the bell, but there was no answer. Since Alan's Mercedes was parked in the circular brick driveway, she knew he was at home. Deciding he must be out in back, swimming laps as he did every evening after a long day perfecting the already glamorous features of movie stars, she took her key from her black satin bag and let herself into the house.

Like the man himself, Alan Sturgess's house exuded cool control. Glass and silver predominated, giving an almost operating room sterility to a living room that had been professionally decorated in shades of gray. Tasteful graphics—nothing too bold or avant-garde—hung on the pale gray walls, illuminated by track lighting along the ten-foot ceiling.

The furniture, like the art, was contemporary. Italian black leather and molded, modular pieces covered in black-and-gray striped upholstery blended perfectly with black lacquer bookshelves and glass-and-chrome tables that seemed to float atop the plush pewter carpeting. A collection of small sculptures was displayed on chrome-and-glass shelves.

An ebony onyx figure of a nude was set atop a black pedestal; when Alan had first revealed that he considered the svelte female figure to be the perfect female form, Blythe, comparing the nude with her own curvaceous body, had felt depressed. Time hadn't changed her feelings.

Refusing to allow herself to be intimidated by an inanimate object, Blythe crossed the room and opened the doors to the terrace. Moonlight created mysterious shadows in the mist that hung over the ocean. The water in the tile-lined pool gleamed a brilliant, crystal clear aquamarine from the underwater light.

She heard the sound of water lapping against the side of the pool. Expecting to see Alan slicing through the warm water with his long, perfect stroke, as she approached the pool, she was surprised to see him in the shadows of the circular steps.

What was even more surprising was that he was not alone.

He had a woman backed up against the cantilevered brick coping. Although his mouth was over hers, and his hands were on her chest, Blythe suspected he was not performing artificial respiration.

Growing aware of her presence a moment after she saw him, he turned. His hands fell to his sides. "Blythe." He recovered quickly. Amazingly, his voice was as cool and collected as always. "I wasn't expecting you."

"I'd say that was more than a little obvious." Using every bit of her acting skills, Blythe kept her tone as calm as his. Anger was bubbling up inside her, like molten lava from a volcano; with Herculean effort, she pushed it down.

He left the pool, allowing Blythe to get her first good look at his companion. Brittany Carlysle had been just another pretty waitress-bit player until Dr. Alan Sturgess had performed his make-over magic on her. Some planing on her nose, a bit of silicone to the cheeks and chin, breast implants and selected liposuction had turned the former University of Texas cheerleader into an up-and-coming sitcom star.

As Brittany stood there, in the shallow end, meeting Blythe's gaze without an ounce of remorse, it occurred to Blythe that Alan had definitely not stuck to his avowed slender ideal. With water wings like that, the starlet would definitely never be in danger of drowning.

Determined to keep things civilized, when she was tempted to throw the champagne bottle she'd almost forgotten she was carrying at her fiancé's head, Blythe said, "I suppose I should apologize for interrupting."

"It's not how it looks." Picking up a towel from a lounge beside the pool, Alan wrapped it around his waist.

"Please." Why was it that the lying irritated her more than the sex? Blythe shook her head. "Don't treat me like a fool, Alan. All three of us know that it's exactly how it looks."

"You're the one who canceled our dinner tonight. Just as you've canceled so many other plans since you became obsessed with making that damn movie about Alexandra Romanov and Patrick Reardon's tawdry tale."

How was it, Blythe wondered, that such a talented, intelligent man could sound like a petulant five-year-old? And how dare he try to turn the blame on her?

"I know. And I was feeling bad about that." She lifted the dark green bottle by its neck. "So I decided to surprise you by saying goodbye in style." Although her voice was calm, her eyes were not. Passion born of fury, not of desire, radiated from every fragrant pore. "But I see I should have called first."

Turning her attention to the television actress, Blythe said, "Hello, Brittany."

"Hi, Blythe." Rather than the embarrassment she would have expected to see, Blythe viewed a certain triumph on the woman's perfect face. "I'm so sorry you had to find out this way."

"Find out?"

"Brittany—" Alan warned, half turning toward her.

"Alan and I have been lovers for months."

"Really?" Blythe arched a sable brow. "Before or after your surgery?"

"Dammit, Brittany, shut up," Alan snapped, in danger of losing his composure for the first time since Blythe's arrival. Which wasn't all that surprising, she considered. Cheating on a fiancée was one thing. Fooling around with a patient could definitely get a physician called before the state medical board.

"Don't worry, Alan." Blythe was not nearly as upset as she should be under the circumstances. "I have no intention of turning you over to the AMA." She turned on a stiletto heel. "Don't bother seeing me out."

"Dammit, don't go." He grasped her arm. "Not yet. We need to talk."

"Really, Alan." She pried his fingers off her bare, night-cooled skin. "What on earth could we possibly have to talk about?"

"Our marriage, of course."

"Marriage?" The man was one surprise after another. "How can you talk about marriage after this?" She cast a disparaging glance toward Brittany, who'd left the pool like Venus rising from her half shell and was currently taking her time climbing into a thong bikini bottom.

"What happened with Brittany has nothing to do with us," Alan insisted. "Or our marriage."

Blythe wondered when she'd become such a bad judge of character. She'd known Alan was judgmental and, given the chance, controlling. She'd accepted the fact that he was stiff and sometimes boring. She'd also gotten used to the idea that not only did he disapprove of her profession, but he was also vehemently opposed to her starting her own production company. He'd also made no secret of the fact that he thought the subject matter of her first independent project was exploitive.

Actually, the word he'd used, on more than one occasion, was *trash*. But at least she'd believed that he was a man of integrity. Obviously, she'd been wrong.

"Are you saying the same thing would have happened if we'd gotten married?"

"Don't be so naive, Blythe." An edge of irritation crept into his tone. "This is Los Angeles. Men sleep with other women every day. And their wives sleep with other men. But that doesn't mean that they can't have a meaningful marriage."

A knot of betrayal and disgust tightened in her gut. "I'm going to try to forget you ever said that." She began walking away again, her long stride sweeping her across the brick, through the still open French doors, into the house.

She was marching across the room when he caught up with her again. "Dammit, you're not being at all reasonable. You've known from the beginning that our marriage wasn't going to be based on any shared passion."

That was precisely what she was doing here tonight. To convince herself otherwise. Blythe paused, mildly curious. "What, exactly was our marriage going to be based on?" she asked coolly. "In your opinion?"

"Mutual success. We're both famous in our own right, Blythe. And wealthy. You know I'm not with you because I want to bed a movie star and I know you're not with me for any financial support or social status."

His fingers curved around her bare shoulders to draw her to him. "Together we can rule this town."

Looking up at him, Blythe was reminded of an old quote about being able to put all the sincerity in Hollywood into a gnat's navel and still have room left over for a sesame seed.

Before she could answer, his head swooped down and he took her mouth in a long hard kiss that tasted of frustration edged with anger.

As she stood still for a kiss she neither wanted nor enjoyed, Blythe suddenly found herself thinking of her parents. Still happily married after thirty years, they held hands while walking on the beach, slow danced cheek to cheek at celebrity fund-raising balls and, if her mother could be believed, continued to neck in the back row of darkened movie theaters.

"As difficult as it will be for you to understand this, Alan," she said, shrugging away from his touch, "I have no interest in grasping or wielding social power and I loathe the idea of being any man's trophy wife."

She began walking toward the front door again. "Have a nice evening."

"Dammit, Blythe, you're making an enormous mistake. If you'd stop being so emotional and listen to reason, you'd see that we can get past this."

"The thing you don't seem to understand, Alan, is that I have no desire to get past this."

As she passed the ebony statue, Blythe was tempted to send it crashing off its pedestal. Determined to retreat with dignity, she resisted the urge.

However, having never claimed to be perfect, she gave in to impulse and slammed the immense mahogany door behind her.

3

AN HOUR LATER, Blythe was sitting on a lounge, out by the pool of the famed Chateau Marmont, staring out over the lights of the city, drinking the exquisite Tattinger.

"There comes a time, in every woman's life," she said, "when the only thing that helps is a glass of champagne." She refilled her glass from the dark green bottle, then held it up to the moonlight to judge the level of champagne remaining. "Bette Davis. In *Now, Voyager*.... No. That's not right."

She shook her head. She knew she was getting a bit tipsy, but at this point, didn't care.

"*Old Acquaintance*, 1943. And she said it to Miriam Hopkins." Having always prided herself on her encyclopedic memory of the movie business, Blythe nodded her satisfaction.

Then tossed back the champagne.

Where the hell was she? Gage slammed the receiver down for the third time that hour. When he hadn't gotten an answer at her hotel bungalow, he'd decided she must have been spending the night with that uptight, socialite nose doctor fiancé. But a call to Alan Sturgess had revealed that although Blythe had been there earlier, she'd returned to the hotel.

There was a flinty edge to the plastic surgeon's tone that suggested all was not going well in the romance sweepstakes. Gage found that idea eminently appealing.

"You're a bastard, Remington," he growled as he began dialing her number again. While he certainly wouldn't wish a broken heart on Blythe, neither did he want her to marry Alan Sturgess.

After several rings, the hotel operator came on the line to tell him what he'd already figured out for himself. That Blythe wasn't answering her phone.

He could, of course, leave a message. But nine years on the force had Gage thinking the worst. Carjackings were becoming more and more common in L.A. A lone woman, driving an expensive car like her Jaguar, was, unfortunately, at risk. Even in the upscale Pacific Palisades neighborhood where Sturgess's house was located. Even at a ritzy place like the Chateau Marmont.

"Hell." He dragged his hand through his hair and considered his options. Then he left Bachelor Arms, and headed up into the hills.

He found her out by the oval swimming pool, staring into the serene blue water.

"You didn't lock the door to your bungalow," he said abruptly, dispensing with any words of greeting. When he'd arrived to find the door unlocked and Blythe gone, he'd suffered a jolt of icy fear. While all the time she'd been drinking champagne out by the pool like the goddamn movie star she was. Her skirt was hitched up, revealing the lacy tops of her thigh-high stockings. The contrast between the jet stockings and creamy porcelain skin caused a low, deep pull that only served to irritate him further.

"I guess I forgot." Blythe didn't question what Gage was doing here. At this point, she was beyond questioning anything.

"She forgot." He shook his head with very real disgust. "Why don't you just send out an invitation to the Manson family while you're at it?"

"They're in prison." Her tongue was thick. Despite childhood elocution lessons, her words were slightly slurred. "I saw him on one of those television newsmagazines not too long ago. He's crazy, you know. Absolutely insane."

She shook her head. "Then again, maybe we're all crazy, living in this town." She polished off another glass and reached for the bottle again.

Gage grabbed it away. "You're drunk, Boss Lady."

"Am I?" She considered that for a long, drawn out moment. "Perhaps just a little." She held out her glass, obviously expecting him to refill it. "But not enough. Not yet."

Having never seen a hint of Blythe having a drinking problem, he wondered what the hell had happened between this afternoon and now.

"Far be it from me to interfere with your little party, but I feel obliged to remind you we have an early flight tomorrow."

"I haven't forgotten." She airily waved her glass. "And for your information, I'm unrelentingly prompt. I have never missed a flight in my life. Are you going to pour me some champagne or not?"

"If you're stupid enough to fly to Europe with a hangover, far be it from me to stop you." He poured a few inches of the sparkling liquid into the Baccarat flute. When she continued to hold her glass out, he muttered a curse and filled it to the crystal rim.

"Thank you." She smiled at him. "You're welcome to help yourself." She crossed her legs with a sensual swish of silk. "Although I'm afraid I only brought one glass outside." She glanced back over her shoulder toward the building. "There are more in my bungalow."

Afraid she'd decide to get up, fall in the pool and drown if he left her out here alone, Gage said, "That's okay. I'll just drink out of the bottle."

"Whatever." When she waved his words away, he noticed something interesting. The diamond that used to weigh down her left hand was missing.

He sat down in the chair beside her, tipped the bottle to his lips and allowed the champagne to slip down his throat. The last time he'd drank sparkling wine had been when he'd graduated from the police academy. But this expensive French vintage was a helluva long way from the cold duck he'd bought at Ralph's supermarket for that occasion. "What are we celebrating?"

"Independence day."

Gage didn't grin. Not on the outside, at any rate. But he wanted to.

"Sounds good to me." He took another drink and decided that although he preferred beer, or the occasional Scotch, this wasn't half-bad.

It was odd, Blythe mused through the haze clouding her mind. Usually being anywhere around this man stirred her up, tangled her emotions and left her feeling nervous and confused. But for some reason, tonight Gage seemed to be having a calming effect on her.

She turned toward him. The dress hitched up a little bit more. "Have you ever been engaged?"

"No." Deciding there was no point in not being totally honest, he added, "I came close once. To a girl I went to college with."

"What happened?"

He shrugged. "It didn't work out." It didn't hurt now because it hadn't hurt then. "We had kind of an unofficial agreement. Then, when I turned down a slot at law school to enroll in the police academy instead, she decided she didn't want to marry a cop."

Blythe looked out over the pool again and sipped her champagne as she considered that. "Sending your husband off to work each day, not knowing if he would be killed, would probably take some getting used to," she said finally, thinking how many times she'd worried about Cait.

"I suppose," Gage agreed. "But that wasn't the reason."

"I don't understand." Her eyes, as they returned to his face, were as wide and dark as a midnight sky. A man could disappear in those eyes, if he wasn't careful. Gage had always considered himself a careful man. "If it wasn't the fear of danger—"

"It was the money." Thinking back on it, Gage realized that it had been his pride, rather than his heart that had been wounded by the broken romance. "Law enforcement isn't all that lucratively rewarding. So she married some hotshot criminal attorney she met while attending a murder trial where I testified for the prosecution. They live in Santa Barbara now.

"In Montecito, actually, in a French regency mansion with a live-in housekeeper, a yard man, a former wannabe actor hunk to clean the pool, and a genuine British nanny for their three kids. Apparently when it comes to the legal profession, crime pays very well.

"In his spare time, he plays golf and screws around. She drinks and screws around."

Gage knew because Sandi Cunningham still called him about three times a year when she was drunk and needy. Having learned his lesson where the woman was con-

cerned, he never took her up on her invitation to get together for old times' sake.

"That's so sad." Goose bumps rose on Blythe's arms
as she thought how close that scenario was to the un-
pleasant marriage plan Alan had sketched out for her
earlier.

"I've always thought so." The night breeze was ruf-
fling the semitropical trees surrounding the pool. Gage
saw her slight shiver and misunderstood its reason. "It's
getting cold. We'd better get you inside. And to bed."

The way he was looking at her made her head spin. Or
perhaps, Blythe thought hopefully, it was the champagne. "So we're back to that."

She'd lifted her chin in a challenging way that dared
him to kiss her. As tempted as he was, Gage feared that
if he allowed himself so much as one little taste, he
wouldn't be able to stop. And besides the fact that making love to a woman in her condition would be uncon-
scionable, he was discovering that he was a selfish man.

When he did make love to Blythe Fielding—and Gage
had every intention of doing exactly that—he wanted to
be damn sure she'd remember it for the rest of her life.

"Back to what?" He stood up, plucked the half-empty
glass from her hand and placed it on the table beside the
bottle.

"You wanting me." She allowed him to help her to her
feet. "Me wanting you."

Even though he knew she wouldn't have made such a
confession under normal conditions, Gage was pleased
by the admission.

"I always want you," he said mildly. She was unsteady on her feet, weaving slightly. And no wonder,
considering how much of that champagne she'd man-

aged to drink before he'd arrived. "But you're safe to-night, Boss Lady."

"Oh." Those remarkable lips that had been taunting his sleep turned down. "What's the matter? Don't you find me attractive?"

One of the skinny little straps had slid off one shoulder, revealing creamy flesh he had a strong, sudden urge to bite. The black silk had been cut to showcase a woman's curves, which it did to distraction. And those hooker heels made her legs look as if they went all the way up to her neck.

"Sweetheart, if you were any more attractive, I'd have to arrest myself for the thoughts I'm having."

"Oh." She smiled, seemingly pleased with that.

"I'm also surprised there isn't a five-day waiting period before buying that dress."

More than pleased, she did a little show-off spin turn that had her wobbling on her spindly high heels. Catching her before she landed in the water, he scooped her up and swung her over his shoulder.

It should definitely be against the law for a woman to smell this good, Gage thought as he marched back through the private gardens to the unlocked bungalow. It should be a felony for a woman to feel this good.

"I always wanted to be swept off my feet," she said on a silvery giggle as he carried her into the bedroom. "But tossing me over your shoulder isn't exactly the most romantic style in the world, Gage. I mean, can you imagine Clark Gable lugging Vivien Leigh up that staircase like a sack of potatoes?"

Hell. He should have known the bedroom would smell like her. Amused, irritated and aroused all at the same time, he dumped her onto the bed.

"You want romance?" he growled as she bounced bonelessly on the mattress.

Fed up with this entire situation that had been driving him crazy for months, he sat down beside her, caught her chin in his tensed fingers and closed his mouth over hers.

Unlike the first time they'd kissed, there was no drawn out exploration, no teasing temptation. Her taste, headier than the French champagne she'd shared, exploded within him. Kissing Blythe was like a cool drink after days spent crawling across hot desert sands, like a warm and welcoming fire after being lost in a blizzard. It was everything he'd remembered. And more. Much, much more.

It would have been easier if she'd resisted. Even for a moment. But instead, she gave without hesitation, throwing herself into the kiss with a desperate passion. Her mouth was like a fever, sending a burst of heat surging through him. Images of smoke and flames sparked in his mind.

Reminding himself of the rules, he tried to back away, but then she was pulling him to her, down onto the bed, urging his body to press her deeper and deeper into the mattress.

She was twined around him, her bare arms, her magnificent legs. Her breasts were flattened by the strength of his chest, her heart thudded fast and hard.

He'd fantasized about this countless times since their first meeting. Experience had taught Gage that reality seldom lived up to the illusion. But with Blythe, amazingly, everything was exactly as he'd imagined.

Gage knew what it was to want a woman. But never in his thirty-one years had he needed a woman like he needed Blythe at this moment. It was as if he'd been searching for her his entire life.

Dragging his mouth away from hers, he skimmed his lips down her throat, lingering at the soft spot where her pulse hammered wildly. The skimpy little straps had slid off both her shoulders; Gage nipped the fragrant flesh with his teeth.

The love bite drew a soft moan from between her parted lips; as he soothed the faint wound with his tongue, Blythe murmured something that could have been either protest or encouragement. Then she arched against him, desperate to be touched. Gage took it for the latter.

Yanking the dress to her waist, he freed first one pale breast from a wispy bit of scarlet silk, then the other. They spilled into his restless hands.

"Oh, yes," she moaned on a shimmering sigh of relief. "More." She felt no embarrassment, only desperation.

As his greedy mouth scorched her burning flesh, as his impatient hands made her burn, Blythe cried out. Here was the passion she'd been seeking, she thought through the smoke and haze clouding her mind. Here was the firestorm she'd never experienced with Alan. Here was the danger she'd been secretly seeking.

Blythe was not inexperienced. She'd known desire. Experienced yearning. But only with Gage had she discovered the true meaning of hunger. Only with Gage had she realized how thin a line there was between want and need.

She tugged his shirt from his jeans with anxious hands; her fingernails dug into his back. The need to feel him against her, inside her, was as urgent, and as necessary, as breath.

He could have her, Gage knew. Now. And despite the wine she'd drunk, he knew that there had been times, with some women, that he wouldn't have hesitated. Because all those glasses of champagne hadn't changed the unalterable fact that he and Blythe had been heading toward this moment for months.

Before, only Alan Sturgess had stood in the way. But now, for whatever reason, the fiancé was gone, out of the picture for good.

So why the hell was he hesitating?

Unable to answer that question, he nevertheless backed away.

"Gage?" Her eyelids fluttered open. Her lips were swollen from his kisses and trembled as a ragged breath slipped through them. Confusion, along with a lingering desire swirled in her liquid-jet eyes, threatening to undermine his resolve yet again.

"I'm sorry." His hands moved to her shoulders. He needed time. Time to steady himself. Time to understand what was happening between them. Time to comprehend why everything about this woman seemed both new and familiar at the same time. "I had no right to do that."

Her lips were unbearably dry. Blythe licked them and saw the blue flames rise in his mesmerizing eyes. "I wanted you to do that," she said in a voice that was barely above a whisper. "I wanted you to kiss me. And touch me." He watched her throat as she swallowed. "I wanted you to make love to me."

Gage groaned inwardly. Here he was, trying to be a hero, and the lady wasn't helping. Not even a little bit.

"I like to know that the woman I'm making love to knows which man she's with."

The accusation cut like a laser through the fog clouding her mind. He could not have said anything that could have hurt her more.

Blythe recoiled as if struck. "If you believe I thought you were Alan—"

"No." Filled with self-disgust, he took one of her suddenly icy hands and lifted it to his lips. "I'm sorry." His eyes, as they met hers over their linked hands offered contrition. "I shouldn't have said that."

Absolutely refusing to cry, Blythe bit her lip. For the second time tonight—the second time in her twenty-five years—she'd been prepared to throw herself at a man. And once again it was turning out to be a disaster.

"You shouldn't have said it," she agreed. She sat up against the pillows and shot him her most quelling look. "You shouldn't have thought it."

Her eyes were liquid pools of hurt and anger, her hair was a sable cloud around her bare shoulders, her skin was a creamy lure that had him second-guessing his misguided attempt at chivalry.

Gage wanted to try to explain but realized he had no answers himself. "Look," he said instead, "you've had a long, tough day and although I believe you about having never missed a flight, that doesn't mean that you shouldn't get some sleep." He reached out and stroked a broad palm down her tousled hair. "Why don't we discuss this tomorrow?"

Even as she wanted to argue, Blythe admitted he had a point. She was suddenly tired. More than tired. Drained.

"I may not be speaking to you tomorrow."

Her haughty tone, a vivid contrast to her warm and sensual appearance, made him smile. "I'll take my chances." He bent his head and brushed his lips across her frowning ones. "Good night, *milaja*," he murmured. And then he was gone.

Lying there, with her head still spinning from a combination of champagne and kisses, Blythe heard him let himself out of the bungalow.

With a muttered curse and a groan, she forced herself to leave the comfort of the bed, undressed, put on a silk nightshirt and brushed her teeth. It was only as she slid beneath the sheets that his last words to her sank in.

Had Gage really called her *sweetheart* in Russian?

Impossible. Just as her knowing the unfamiliar word was impossible. Sighing, Blythe closed her eyes and drifted off on soft swells toward sleep, the endearment, and the puzzle, forgotten.

"YOU'RE LATE," *Alexandra accused.*

Patrick stood in the doorway to the bathroom, gazing at her, lounging in the hedonistic black marble tub, up to her lissome neck in fragrant bubbles, looking every bit the luscious sex goddess she was. She'd piled her thick hair atop her head in a riot of dark curls. A few tendrils trailed wetly down her neck, contrasting enticingly with her alabaster skin.

Her eyes were thickly lashed, as dark as a midnight sky over the Russian steppes. Those full lips, currently pouting prettily, were naturally the hue of ripe raspberries, which allowed her to forego messy lipstick except when she was about to go before the cameras.

Alexandra Romanov was every red-blooded male's sensual fantasy. And she was his.

Ten months after their marriage, there were still times when Patrick found that idea overwhelming.

"I'm sorry." He unfastened the cuffs of his shirt. "I got held up at the studio."

As he entered the steamy bathroom, he was immediately surrounded by a fragrant cloud. It was the same

*scent that she smoothed all over her body each morning
and evening. Only last night, he'd been the one to spread
the lush pink cream over her silken flesh.*

He grew hard as he remembered the uninhibited way
she'd pressed against his hand as he lingered over the skin
at the inside of her milky thighs, remembered the way
she'd first pleaded, then cried out in Russian.

"I hate Walter Stern." She called the studio head a nasty
name in her native language as she lifted a lithe leg out
of the water and began washing it with a pink bar of
French milled soap.

"You and half the western world."

His relationship with the man who'd brought him to
Los Angeles, while never exactly friendly, had at least
been cordial. Since he'd infuriated Stern by eloping with
the studio's biggest star, their working alliance had
nearly disintegrated entirely.

Walter continued to insist, to anyone who would listen—including those two gossip harridans Hedda Hop-
per and Louella Parsons—that marriage had damaged
Alexandra's sex appeal, in turn endangering Xanadu's
profits.

Personally, Patrick believed that Stern's real problem
was a deep-seated jealousy that he wasn't the man sharing Alexandra's bed every night.

"So what exactly did Walter want now?" Alexandra
asked.

"I don't know." He dismissed the anxiety in her voice.
She worried too much. Patrick supposed that came from
being Russian.

Lord knows—though she'd never revealed much about
her past—if the newsreels coming out of that country
were even halfway reliable, her earlier life back home in
her native country couldn't have been easy.

He shrugged out of his shirt, tossing it uncaringly into a corner. "I waited around for a while, then, when he didn't show up, I came home. To my wife."

"I'm glad you did." She changed legs. Luminescent bubbles clung to her firm calves. Her lacquered toenails gleamed like rubies. *"I was getting lonely. And impatient."* As intended, his gaze followed the glistening bar of soap from ankle to thigh. *"So I had no choice but to start without you."*

"Don't worry, I have every intention of catching up."

He sat down on the silly pink velvet stool the decorator had placed in front of the gilt-framed mirror and pulled off his boots, one at a time. Then he stood up again and went to work on his pants.

Watching her watch him unfasten the five metal buttons at the front of his jeans made Patrick feel a lot like the Black Angus breeding bull he kept back on his ranch in Wyoming.

One of the things he loved about Alexandra was that from the first moment they'd met, she hadn't bothered to play coy. She'd wanted him every bit as much as he'd wanted her. And hadn't been afraid to let him know it. On the contrary, as they'd wrestled in the back seat of his Rolls, twenty minutes after meeting, Patrick figured it would always be a toss-up as to who seduced whom.

Her expressive brown eyes darkened to nearly black as she gazed with uncensored desire at his erection. Her lips curved into a slow, womanly smile. When she licked her lips, his blood burned. *"Is that for me?"*

"Later." Naked now, he knelt beside the tub, picked up the bath sponge and dipped it into the velvet cling of water. *"Much, much later."*

With that erotic promise hovering in the air between them, Patrick proceeded to wash every inch of her lush,

*voluptuous body. The water cooled even as her flesh
warmed. Alexandra was the most responsive woman
he'd ever met, the only female he knew who could be
brought to orgasm by kissing her breasts, or nipping at
the cord at the back of her knee, or even touching the tip
of his tongue at that soft spot behind her earlobe.*

*"Enough!" Laughing, crying, cursing in her native
language, she used all her strength to pull him into the
tub with her.*

*And as he slid into her with a silky wet ease, he con-
sidered, not for the first time since moving into the house,
that Alexandra Romanov Reardon was his every wish
come true.*

4

FEELING AS IF he were about to explode, Gage was jerked out of a restless sleep. His aching body was rock hard. And frustrated.

"Damn." Groaning, he climbed out of bed and made his way painfully into the kitchen where he poured a glass of ice water. As he chugged it down, then followed it with another, he willed it to cool his lingering physical hunger.

This was getting ridiculous. If he wasn't suffering hot dreams about Blythe, he was having them about Alexandra.

"The problem, pal," he decided as he put the empty glass into the dishwasher, "is it's been too long since you got laid."

Since the day he'd first met Blythe Fielding, he hadn't wanted any other woman. Reminding himself that he'd always been known for his patience, Gage told himself that Blythe was worth waiting for.

He was still telling himself that as he crossed the living room on the way back to bed. As so often happened since moving into the apartment that also served as his office, his gaze was unwillingly drawn to the oversize pewter mirror.

"Aw, hell." He dragged both hands down his face and told himself the vision was only a leftover fantasy from his earlier dream.

But it wasn't. When he looked into the silver-backed glass again, he knew, deep in his gut, that the ethereal ebony-haired woman clad in the pale, flowing gown was, at least on some level, all too real.

Unsurprised, since everything else in his life had gone haywire lately, he returned the sober gaze with the same no-nonsense stare that had always worked well for him on the street.

"Well?" he challenged grumpily. "Which is it going to be? Are you here to grant my greatest wish? Or am I going to experience my worst fear?"

He wasn't surprised when she didn't answer. He hadn't expected her to.

"You know, I really don't need this," he complained. "Not now. See, in the first place, I'm a little busy these days. Not that I'm complaining about having too much work, understand, because I'm not.

"But along with the rest of my cases, this Alexandra Romanov investigation is turning out to be a real bitch. I mean, nothing about it is turning out to be predictable. Or easy."

Including Blythe, he tacked on mentally, wondering idly if the lovely phantom with the sad eyes could read minds. "In the second place, I've already got two fantasy women driving me up a wall. I'm not certain I can handle another.

"So, no insult intended, sweetheart, but why don't you just fade away to wherever the hell it is you phantoms go, and try some other time?"

Again, there was no answer. But, as Gage watched, her lips turned into a slow smile. Then, as requested, she faded away.

"You realize of course," Gage told himself gruffly, "that you're losing it."

Glancing over at the clock, he saw there was only another two hours left before he had to leave for the airport. Needing to work off his lingering sexual frustration before being in forced proximity to the woman who was driving him around the bend, he pulled on running shorts, a ragged LAPD T-shirt and a pair of Nike Air Jordan shoes.

He left the apartment and ran a five-mile circuit throughout the neighborhood. Then, for good measure, he ran another three miles.

When he returned home, the pink Mediterranean apartment was bathed in the golden glow of a morning sunrise. His heart was pounding against his ribs, his blood was flowing, he was drenched in sweat and his clothes clung wetly to his body.

Unfortunately, the enforced exercise had failed to drive Blythe—or the equally luscious Alexandra—from his mind.

He wanted her. Just as she wanted him. And although he wasn't certain he could handle the consequences, he knew that the time would soon come to move their relationship to the next step.

It was only logical, especially now that she was no longer committed to Sturgess, that they would make love on this trip. Striving for the logic that had always served him well, Gage knew the odds were that during their time in Greece, the passion that had burned between Blythe and him from the beginning would flare itself out. It was, he told himself, the logical conclusion.

The only problem was, there was nothing remotely logical about his feelings for this woman.

IT WAS THE GLARE of early morning sunshine streaming in through the window that woke her. Feeling as if her head were filled with rocks, Blythe moaned and pulled the pillow over her head.

"Rise and shine," Gage said cheerily.

"Go away," she muttered from beneath the goose down pillow.

"I could. But then you'd undoubtedly break your record of never missing a plane."

The idea of spending hours on an overseas flight made her moan. "Why didn't you stop me last night?"

Understanding she was referring to her overindulgence, Gage decided against mentioning that he had, with effort, stopped them both from something far more dangerous than too much champagne.

"You'd already made inroads on the bottle by the time I arrived," he reminded her mildly. "I suggested you might want to go easy, but you seemed to have a different goal in mind."

"I was trying to drown Alan," she said as the memory of finding her fiancé with another woman came back to her.

"I kind of figured that out for myself. If you'd asked, I could have told you that it doesn't work."

She pushed the pillow aside and opened her scratchy lids. Having achieved that much, she tried sitting up and cringed as the boulders in her head began tumbling around.

"Tried to drown a lot of women with booze, have you?" She licked her arid lips with a tongue that felt like sandpaper.

"Only one." He leaned down and pushed her tumbled hair away from her face with one hand and held a glass out to her with the other. "It left me with a hangover about like the one you're suffering now. And you know what?"

"What?"

"I still haven't managed to get you out of my mind."

The admission, which she knew was not some practiced line to coax her into his bed, was too much for Blythe to handle this morning. The slow burn that she always felt when this man was anywhere in the vicinity had become so mixed up with a confusion of fantasies and dreams that she was losing track of what was real and what was imagined.

"Gage—"

"Don't worry." His smile was warm and nonthreatening. As was his hand as he stroked her hair. "I'm not about to push, Blythe. Not until you're ready." And from her pasty complexion and red-rimmed eyes, Gage knew it was going to be awhile. "Here. Drink this. It'll help."

She looked at the rust-colored liquid with suspicion. "What is it?"

"An old family recipe for hangovers."

"It looks like toxic waste."

"Kinda tastes like it, too," he said agreeably. "But it works." His coaxing smile was enough to almost ease her headache. "Trust me."

She did, Blythe realized. With more than a hangover cure. Taking the glass from his outstretched hand, she took a tentative sip. "Ugh." The taste was enough to make anyone give up drinking forever. "What's in this, anyway?"

"You don't want to know." He grinned. "Come on, Boss Lady. Down the hatch. I've got coffee brewing for afterward."

Squeezing her eyes shut, she clutched the glass in both hands and swallowed the unsavory mixture down in rapid gulps. "I think I'm going to die," she complained, flopping back against the pillows and closing her eyes. "Then again I'm afraid I might not."

Unable to resist the lure of her too pale face, he sat down on the bed and ran the back of his hand up her cheek. "He wasn't worth it."

"I know." She flung a hand over her eyes. "It was stupid. But I was so damn mad."

"Mad?" Having seen the headache in her eyes, he began rubbing his fingers in slow, soothing circles against her temples.

Blythe could hear the question in his voice, even through the racket from the maniacs who were pounding away with jackhammers inside her head. "I don't want to talk about it. Not now."

"Fine." He bent down and pressed a light kiss against her furrowed brow. "As you've pointed out on numerous occasions, you're the boss."

Before she could discern his intentions, Gage scooped her from the bed and carried her into the adjoining bathroom. He considered stripping off her silk nightshirt, then decided he could only be expected to resist so much temptation. Still holding her in his arms, he reached into the shower and turned on the water.

"Dammit, Gage!" Blythe shouted as he stuck her beneath the stream of water. "What do you think you're doing?"

"Making sure we catch our plane." Knowing it would get her blood stirring even more, he gave her a quick pat on the rear, trying not to notice how the wet emerald green silk clung to her firm buttocks. "You'll thank me for this when we've tracked down Natasha."

"If I don't kill you first," Blythe muttered in response.

She didn't speak more than two words to him during the entire flight to New York. But since she'd spent those hours reclining in her first-class seat with her eyes closed, Gage figured her lack of conversation was due as much to the lingering aftereffects of too much champagne as to her irritation at his admittedly chauvinistic behavior that morning.

He was right. By the time they'd landed at Kennedy, and taken the shuttle to the international terminal, Blythe was beginning, almost, to feel like a human being again.

"I'm starving," she announced after they'd checked the flight information screen and learned their plane would be delayed an hour.

"I'm not surprised. You haven't eaten a thing all day." She'd passed up the seemingly continual meal service, but he had managed to talk her into eating the bread stick that had come with his smoked salmon pasta.

"I was afraid to put anything on top of that unappetizing glop you made me drink this morning."

"You're still alive," he pointed out. "And your color's coming back." He leaned down and took off the sunglasses she'd been wearing since they left the hotel six hours earlier. "And your eyes don't look like road maps anymore."

"As filthy tasting as it was, I can't deny that I'm feeling better," she admitted. "Good enough, in fact, for a burger and fries."

"In this place?" He glanced around the terminal with obvious disdain.

"We don't exactly have time to run into Manhattan for an early supper at 21."

"Got a point there."

One of the things Gage especially liked about Blythe was the way, even though she'd been born into wealth, she lacked any tendency toward caste snobbery. He'd also never been fond of women who accepted a date to dinner, then picked at the entrée, perhaps eating one or two birdlike bites. Sometimes he had the feeling every female on the planet was on a diet. Every female but Blythe.

"You *were* hungry," he commented, after having watched her make a cheeseburger, an order of greasy fries, a Coke and a rock-hard brownie disappear.

"Starved," she repeated. Amazingly, the food seemed to have done the trick. She was, for the first time today, feeling almost human. "But then again, I've always had this horrendous appetite. I keep telling myself that I should watch my weight, but then I get a craving, and I cave in."

"I like a woman who caves in to cravings." There was a bright spot of catsup on the corner of her mouth. Dipping a corner of the paper napkin into his water glass, Gage wiped it away. "As for watching your weight, why don't we just add that to my job description?"

His eyes took a long, slow look at her perched on the stool at the counter. "Although it probably isn't fair, me charging you for the job. When looking at your body is one of my all-time favorite things to do."

It was happening again! The hustle and bustle of the crowded terminal faded into the background; the voices, speaking in myriad native tongues, the flight announcements, the no-parking warning, all became a distant buzz. She and Gage could have been the only two people in the terminal. In the world. On the planet.

"We'd better get to our gate." Was that really her voice? Blythe wondered with amazement. So calm, so matter-of-fact?

"I suppose so." Reaching out, he touched her hair, lightly, only his fingers to the sable tips. "You really are so incredibly lovely."

His mesmerizing silvery blue eyes were painfully seductive. The unthreatening contact was almost more than she could handle. The emotions Gage always seemed to bring out in her were neither safe nor comfortable. But, she feared, inevitable.

"Even with a hangover?" she asked with deliberate casualness that didn't fool Gage for a moment. She drew back, freeing herself from his light touch.

"Even then. Always."

Although an airport snack bar was not conducive to private conversations, Blythe couldn't let such an outrageous declaration go unchallenged.

"You disappoint me, Gage." When his only response was to lift a brow, she elaborated. "I'd hoped you were different. That you were not just another man who couldn't see beyond the Hollywood image."

He laughed at that—a rough, humorless sound—because when they'd first met, he'd found himself actually disliking the Blythe Fielding of the Hollywood image.

It was when he'd realized that she was much more than just another beautiful face, that she possessed an incredible amount of depth beneath that voluptuous body designed for sin and sexual fantasies, that he'd known he was in deep, deep trouble.

She stiffened. "I didn't realize I'd said anything that funny."

Hell. He hadn't meant to hurt her. Gage's expression sobered. "You didn't." His tone was soft, his gaze calm and deep and tender. "Not really."

Blythe had the strangest feeling that Gage had known her all her life, was intimate with all her flaws, and loved her anyway.

No. Not *love*. *Want*. There was, Blythe reminded herself sternly, an enormous difference.

"I'll admit to having wanted you almost from the moment I saw you," he said, unknowingly confirming her thoughts. "I also want you more with every minute—every day—that passes. But I also care for you, Blythe. More than I'd planned. A helluva lot more than I should."

Her right hand was in her lap. He covered it with his. "*You*. Not Xanadu Studios' larger-than-life movie star, but the intelligent, warmhearted, and yes, incredibly sexy woman beneath all the glitter and hype."

He said it so simply it could only be the truth. Exaggeration wasn't Gage's style, Blythe knew. He was straightforward and honest to a fault. She could only guess how much it cost him to be so unflinchingly open with her now.

She turned her hand and linked their fingers together. She didn't say a word. None were needed.

HOURS LATER, after they'd finally landed in Athens, Gage telephoned his Greek counterpart, who'd been keeping track of Natasha's whereabouts.

"She's left Seriphos," he told Blythe, who was waiting with their luggage in an airport lounge.

"Terrific." She dragged her hand through her hair. "If you tell me she's on her way back to America, I'm going to throw myself off the top of the nearest temple."

Despite having napped briefly during the overseas flight, she was tired, and it showed. There were shadows beneath her dark eyes and the color she'd regained

after eating that hamburger in New York had faded away
again. But she could still not be anything but stunning.
Her exquisite bone structure assured that she would still
be beautiful when she was Natasha Kuryan's age.

"We're in luck." Tempted to kiss her frown into a smile,
he took her hand and kissed each finger, one at a time.
"The yacht she's visiting on was docked in Mykonos."

"Was?"

"They're on their way to Aegina." He brushed his lips
over her knuckles. "They're expected in a few hours." He
touched his mouth to the inside of her wrist. Her pulse
was fast, but steady. "While we can be there in thirty
minutes."

Blythe was exhausted and frustrated, and the way he
was tangling her already-raw nerves wasn't helping. "So
what are we supposed to do while we wait?" she asked
petulantly.

"Find a place to stay. Have a bite to eat. A nap, perhaps." He bent his head and gave her a sweet, brief kiss.
"After that, I have several suggestions." His slow, seductive smile could have charmed the mythical Greek
sorceress Circe out of her magic spells.

"I'll just bet you do." She might be aroused, but she
was also too intelligent to allow Gage to keep looking at
her that way, touching her that way, dear Lord, kissing
her that way in such a public place. She rose from the
hard plastic chair. "Let's go. Right now a real bed sounds
like nirvana."

Gage picked up the suitcases, putting one under each
arm. "My thought exactly," he drawled.

In the fifth century, B.C., the ancient port of Piraeus
had been home to the galleys of Themistocles' great
Athenian fleet. Today, sleek white yachts and cruises
were moored in the sheltered bays. Foregoing the lum-

bering car ferries, Blythe and Gage boarded one of the yellow-and-blue hydrofoils.

As it literally bounded over the rough water, Blythe decided that the name, *Flying Dolphin*, definitely fit. And although she'd never been prone to seasickness, she was definitely grateful that Gage's horrid concoction had calmed her queasy stomach.

Named for one of Zeus's conquests, the island of Aegina was bathed in a benevolent gold sunlight.

Whitewashed houses covered the nearby hillsides in a haphazard series of terraces, their tile roofs blanched by sun and years to a pale, pinkish glow. The doors and window frames were painted in scintillating scarlets, sapphire blues and brilliant emerald greens. "It's absolutely charming," she breathed as they disembarked.

"You sound as if you've never been here before." Gage led her past the colorful vegetable market boats moored at the dock to one of the horse-drawn carriages waiting dockside. A taxi would have been more practical, but what he was feeling had nothing to do with practicality. "I thought you told me you'd been to Greece."

"I have, a long time ago. But I was working on a film and never made it to this island." While she waited for Gage to help the driver load their luggage, Blythe secretly enjoyed the obvious compliment called to her by one of a trio of Greek sailors.

"When I was fifteen, I went to Crete," she said after he'd helped her up into the high seat. "We were there on location for three weeks, filming one of those summer teen movies. Sort of an updated, foreign *Beach Blanket Bingo*."

Her smile was brighter than the Mediterranean sunshine. Gage was extremely grateful to the absent Natasha for bringing them to this unabashedly romantic spot.

"Must have been fun."

"It was." Color flooded into her cheeks at the ten-year-old memory. "There was this drop-dead gorgeous waiter at the hotel. His name was Nikos. Nikos Dasskalakis."

When he felt a surge of something that could only be jealousy at the way her voice softened on the long-ago waiter's name, Gage knew he was losing it.

"Lucky Nikos."

She heard the edge to Gage's tone, wondered if he could possibly be jealous, and found herself rather enjoying the idea.

"Remembering back, I realize that I made a horrible pest of myself. I flirted with him outrageously, tried every feminine wile I could think of, but although he was funny and nice, I could tell he didn't really consider me nearly as grown-up as I considered myself."

Her soft smile was directed inward. "Finally, the night before I had to return to the States, in an act of pure teenage desperation, I followed him home. I had this crazy idea that I'd hide in the shadows until he went to bed, then sneak into his house and show him exactly how mature I could be."

Gage linked their hands together, pleased when she didn't pull away. "So, what happened? Did Nikos fall under your youthful, seductive spell?"

Blythe laughed. A deep, rich, musical sound that pulled a thousand hidden chords deep inside Gage. "I discovered he didn't live alone. The woman was about ten years older than me, and worlds sexier.

"They hadn't closed the shutters and as I watched her greet him with a kiss hotter than anything I'd ever seen in the movies, I realized I was definitely in over my head, so I returned to the hotel where I spent the rest of the night crying into my pillow."

"But you survived."

"Of course." Her friendly tone hardened. "I always have."

Their eyes touched and Gage knew they were no longer talking about her youthful crush on that Greek waiter.

"There's something I need to know," he said. "About last night."

Blythe stiffened involuntarily at the memory. Unwilling to look at him, she dragged her gaze away, pretending sudden interest in a clutch of elderly widows. They were uniformly swathed in black, as if in denial of the bright and cheery sunshine. One of the women was baking bread in an outdoor oven.

She shook her head. "I told you, I don't want to talk about that."

"I know. And I also know that it's technically none of my business. But there's one thing that's been driving me crazy ever since I found you drinking your way through that champagne last night. Ever since I kissed you and you kissed me back. Kissed me as if you really meant it."

He cupped her face in his hand and gave her a long look. "Was it just one of those short-lived lovers' spats? Or is it really over?"

Cait had once told her that Gage's confession rate had been one of the highest in the department. If this look was the one he'd used while interrogating suspects, she could understand his success. Because it was certainly working on her.

"It's over."

He read the truth in her eyes. But it wasn't quite enough. "One more thing—"

"Really, Gage—"

"Humor me." His fingers stroked her cheek. "Please?"

Along with his interrogation success, Blythe had heard enough about Gage's days on the L.A. police force to know that he was one of the toughest, strongest men she'd ever meet. She suspected he was not accustomed to begging anyone for anything.

"What do you want to know?"

"Did you break it off? Or did he?"

"I did."

"Because of something the guy did? Or because you decided you didn't want to go through life as the wife of a stuffed-shirt, egotistical, social-climbing snob?"

Deciding to get the truth out in the open, once and for all, Blythe said, "All right. I'm going to tell you what happened last night. Then I never want to hear the man's name again."

"Suits me." Personally, Gage wouldn't mind if another earthquake hit right beneath the doctor's house and swallowed the bastard up.

For the next few minutes, as the cart weaved its way through the narrow, curving streets, Blythe told Gage all about her initial reasons for wanting to marry Alan, about her recent doubts, about her decision to go there last night and prove to herself that her fears were only ordinary premarital jitters, as she'd hoped.

She also related how she'd found Alan with Brittany. And, how, when she'd tried to leave, the man she'd come so close to spending the rest of her life with, had assured her that his infidelity need not interfere with their pending marriage.

"He even had the nerve to try to blame it on me."

Gage was not surprised. Although he'd known it was highly unethical, he'd investigated Sturgess after meeting Blythe and had discovered that other women routinely spent the night at the doctor's home.

He'd considered telling Blythe about her fiancé's behavior innumerable times over the past months, but had decided that when she did come to him, he wanted her to come on her own volition.

"So the guy's a two-timing creep," he said now with a forced shrug. "You're lucky to have found out before you walked down that aisle again."

The statement struck a deep-seated chord. Their eyes met and Blythe knew that once again they were thinking the same thing. Her heart began thrumming painfully as she looked up at him, remembering how, as she'd walked down the aisle on the way to exchange wedding vows with Alan, her mind had inexplicably tangled with Gage's, exchanging words neither of them had even known they'd been thinking.

You can't do this, his stormy eyes had told her.

I have to, hers had answered back. She'd been, Blythe remembered now, inexplicably close to tears.

You don't have to do anything, his had countered on a flare of passion. *But leave with me. Now.*

I can't.

You can. He'd held her desperate gaze to his with the sheer strength of his not inconsiderable will. *I'll help you.*

They hadn't said a single word out loud. But it hadn't been necessary. And although, up until that moment, from the day she'd hired him to unearth information about Alexandra Romanov and Patrick Reardon, their relationship had remained strictly business, Blythe had found herself unreasonably tempted.

Before she could take Gage up on his outrageous demand, the earthquake had struck, shattering the suspended moment.

Now, as she sat beside him in the horse-drawn carriage on this lovely, sun-drenched island, Blythe knew that whatever happened between her and Gage, she owed him the truth.

"There's something you need to know," she said quietly.

The silence swirled around them. Blythe swallowed. "I went there last night, with that bottle of champagne, to seduce Alan."

It was definitely not what Gage had wanted to hear. But still he waited.

Blythe watched Gage carefully, unable to see a flicker of emotion in his expression. For not the first time, she envied him the ability to keep his thoughts to himself. Despite a lifetime of acting, it was a talent she'd never been able to perfect. Even now, she knew her emotions were undoubtedly written across her face in bold script.

"I wanted—no, I needed—to prove something to myself."

She paused, waiting again for some response. And although he still didn't say a word, she thought she saw a hint of encouragement in his steady gaze.

His fingers were still splayed against her cheek; Blythe placed her own hand on the side of his face, rewarded when she felt a muscle tense.

"I needed to find out," she admitted on a low, throaty voice, "whether I could feel for Alan what I've felt for you from the beginning."

The tension left Gage like air from a balloon.

"Do you have any idea," he asked, his own voice rough and husky with unmasked hunger, "how long I've been waiting to hear you say that to me?"

"Yes." Her lips trembled. Moisture filled her expressive dark eyes. "Every bit as long as I've been afraid to say it to you. Or to myself."

Overwhelmed with emotion, she closed her eyes. When she opened them again, Gage was able to read myriad emotions—relief, desire, and concern—in those dazzling dark depths.

"So. Where do we go from here?" she asked quietly.

"I don't know."

The obvious answer was to bed, but Gage knew she was not talking about the immediate future. He wanted, more than he'd ever wanted anything in his life, to sweep her into his arms, cover her uplifted face with kisses and swear a lifetime of bliss. But the need to be honest with her kept him cautious.

Because it had been too long since he'd kissed her, Gage lowered his head and touched his mouth to hers.

5

His kiss, gentle as it was, made her breathless. His hands, as they caressed her shoulders, warmed her all the way to the bone.

"How about we play it by ear?" he suggested, plucking at her soft lips with his.

"That's probably the best thing to do," Blythe agreed on a soft, rippling sigh as he circled her parted lips with the tip of his tongue. "For now."

"For now," Gage agreed roughly.

Neither spoke the rest of the way to the hotel. It was enough just to be in each other's company.

Despite being so close to the hustle and bustle of Athens, the tiny island of Aegina possessed a quiet country charm. As their carriage passed a curly-haired boy who looked as if he might ride a dolphin to school, leading a herd of goats up into the hills, Blythe felt her fatigue and tension melting away.

The hotel was located atop a hill, looking out over the cerulean blue sea. The dazzling white walls were hung with brilliant purple and crimson bursts of bougainvillea and hibiscus. The central courtyard was dominated by a huge stone fountain.

"This is truly delightful," she enthused, drinking in the fragrance of the thick-vined wisteria and orange and lemon trees. "How on earth did you know about it?"

"Since we didn't know where Natasha would finally light, before we left, Connor gave me a list of the best hotels on each of the islands."

It was, Blythe knew, exactly the sort of thing Connor Mackay would do. The fact that this particular hotel was unabashedly romantic, suggested Lily's husband-to-be had joined his wife's and Cait's ongoing matchmaking campaign.

"You realize of course," Gage said, proving once again his uncanny ability to read her mind, "that they're all expecting us to finally make love on this trip."

"I know."

They were climbing a steep, narrow path of polished and worn limestone. Gage stopped and looked down at her. "You also realize, don't you, that they're not alone?"

She looked up at him, her answer shining in her lustrous eyes. "I know."

He breathed out a long, relieved sigh. "Do you have any idea how much I want to book us into a room, then drag you immediately off to bed and spend the rest of the day ravishing your delectable body?"

The idea definitely had merit. Slanting him her most provocative glance, Blythe asked, "What's stopping you?"

Did she have any idea what it did to a man? Gage wondered, when she looked up at him, those remarkable dark gypsy eyes overbrimming with sensual female invitation. Of course she did, he answered his own question. She was, after all, an extremely talented actress. Even so, he knew she was not feigning her desire.

He laughed. A rough, harsh sound that was part pleasure, part pain. "How about the fact that I've been waiting too damn long for this not to do it right?"

Gage drew her into a hidden alcove beneath the shade of an orange tree covered with fragrant white blossoms. "How would you like to help me live out a fantasy?"

She twined her arms around his neck. "I can't think of anything I'd rather do," she said truthfully.

Gage decided that sweeter words had never been spoken. Unable to resist the lure of those silky, succulent lips, he kissed her again, a long, deep kiss that left them both aching.

"I want you to get dressed up in your sexiest dress." A thought occurred to him. "You did bring one, didn't you?"

Having known all along how this trip would turn out, Blythe had come prepared. That being the case, she refused to be coy. "Of course."

Gage liked the fact that she wasn't the type of woman to play sexual games, wondered if she would prove this honest in bed and decided that with him, at least, she would.

"Then I want to take you out on the town," he said, continuing the scenario. "For a long candlelit dinner under the stars, complete with champagne and a crazy Gypsy violinist who'll play passionate romantic ballads while I play with your leg beneath the tablecloth."

She'd had much the same fantasy herself. Today, in fact, while she'd pretended to be sleeping on the plane. "It sounds like a wonderful evening."

"Believe me, sweetheart, I'm just getting started." He ran his hand down her hair and imagined, not for the first time, what those silky dark strands would feel like splayed across his chest. "After dinner, I want to take you dancing. I want to hold you in my arms and whisper mad, passionate promises into your ear."

She let out a long breath. "Oh, I like that part."

He lowered his head until his lips were a mere whisper from hers. "I rather thought you might."

Feeling freer than she had in weeks, in months, she tilted her head back and laughed. "And then what?"

He framed her smiling face between his palms, smoothing his thumbs up over her cheekbones to her temples. "How about a long, moonlit walk along the beach?"

His tender touch caused her blood to hum. "Better and better," Blythe said a little breathlessly. "What next?"

He envisioned taking her back to her room, where he'd slowly take that sexy dress off her, kissing every inch of warm, fragrant flesh.

He would touch her everywhere. Taste her. All over. As she would touch him. Taste him.

Then finally, after they'd driven one another absolutely crazy, he'd bury himself in her soft, welcoming body and make love to her all night long.

And then he'd start all over again.

His burning gaze moved over her with exquisite slowness, leaving sparks wherever it touched. His hands moved down her neck, across her shoulders, down her arms.

Linking their fingers together, he drew her closer, until her breasts were touching the rigid muscle of his chest and her firm thighs melded against his.

"How about we just let nature take its course?" he suggested.

His gaze, his heated words, his tantalizing touch, all conspired to make her almost forget exactly why they'd come to Greece in the first place.

"What about Natasha?" she felt obliged to ask, in a weak voice ragged with her own need.

"From what I've heard, she's got her own man." She was so beautiful, Gage thought. And so sweet. And now, amazingly, with Sturgess out of the picture, Blythe was all his. And whatever happened with this investigation, he had no intention of letting her get away.

"She certainly hasn't stayed in any one place more than a few days since she came to Greece on that cruise," Blythe pointed out. "What if she leaves again before we get a chance to ask her about Alexandra and Patrick?"

"Good point." He reluctantly put her a little bit away. "We'll interview her as soon as the yacht docks. Then afterward, whatever happens, whatever the lady has to say about our star-crossed lovers, I'm taking you out to dinner."

"Yes."

"And dancing."

She could no longer deny this man anything. "Yes."

"And then afterwards—"

"Oh, yes." Going up on her toes, Blythe pressed her smiling lips against his. The kiss was sweet and long and delicious. "Yes, yes, yes! To everything."

"THE LOVEBIRDS have landed."

Although the lobby was deserted, the man, who'd been following Gage and Blythe since boarding the plane with them in Los Angeles, kept his voice low as he placed the overseas call to his employer. "Of course they haven't seen me. They're too wrapped up in each other to notice anything.

"You know, I'm almost feeling guilty about throwing a monkey wrench into Remington's plans. From the way the chick's all over him, it's obvious that he's about to get lucky."

His cigarette-roughened voice let out a sound that was more bark than laugh. Deep creases appeared in his scarred face as he grinned wickedly.

"Don't worry." His voice hardened at the censure coming from L.A. As did his dark eyes. "He's bound to leave her alone sometime before tomorrow. That's when I'll make my move."

As he hung up the phone, the man, one of those lucky individuals who truly enjoyed his work, smiled with anticipation.

SINCE IT WAS TOO EARLY for dinner, especially in a country where the restaurants didn't open until at least nine, after checking into the hotel—taking two adjoining rooms to alleviate temptation—Gage and Blythe decided to pass the time sight-seeing. Although it was not their first choice, by unspoken agreement, both knew that anticipation could be a potent aphrodisiac.

Not that any was needed, Blythe thought as Gage drove their rented jeep through the narrow, winding streets to the famed temple of the Grecian nymph Aphia. Even the sight of his dark hands on the steering wheel caused her to imagine them on her body. And to ache with need.

They passed tavernas where old men sat outside in the sunshine at rickety tables, drinking coffee and playing *tavli*—backgammon. And countless churches, freshly whitewashed in celebration of the recently passed Easter week.

The temple crowned a hilltop overlooking the Saronic Gulf.

"It says here," Blythe read from the guide book they'd bought in town, "that this temple, along with the Parthenon and the Poseidon temple in Sounion, forms an equilateral triangle."

"Fascinating," Gage said.

But his attention was not on the stone ruins but on Blythe. She'd changed from the linen slacks and silk blouse she'd worn for traveling into a calf-length, hibiscus red dress that bared her arms and clung enticingly to her legs. Until this moment, Gage had never realized exactly how sexy a woman's calves could be.

She heard the hunger in his voice, looked up from the page, and although his eyes were shielded by the dark lenses of his sunglasses, she could literally feel the desire radiating from him.

"I was referring to the temple."

Gage shrugged. "You know what they say about beauty being in the eyes of the beholder." And Blythe was, without a doubt, the most beautiful sight on any continent.

Although she was no longer some naive schoolgirl, Blythe felt herself blushing. Dragging her attention back to the text, she said, "The missing sculptures were purchased in 1813 by King Ludwig I of Bavaria.... Gage, are you listening?"

"I'm hanging on every word," he assured her, even as he found himself wondering what she was wearing beneath that clinging crimson dress.

"You're the one who suggested sight-seeing."

"Don't remind me. It seemed like a good idea at the time." He dragged his hand through his hair. "But that was before I discovered what time Greeks ate dinner."

"We could always change our plans."

For some strange reason he could not comprehend, he found himself thinking of how Patrick and Alexandra had reportedly made love within minutes of meeting.

And although he and Blythe had been leading up to this night for months, Gage found himself wanting to make it one she'd remember for the rest of her life. One they'd both remember. What he wanted, he realized, was the kind of romantic interlude they'd someday tell their grandchildren about. Heavily censored, of course.

"It's only a few more hours. I suppose I can hold out. If you can."

Blythe laughed. "Far be it from me to ruin your fantasy."

He grinned at that, a quick, sexy grin that made her heart turn somersaults. "Don't worry. As it happens, where you're concerned, I've got a million of them."

He was not, Blythe thought, alone in that regard. Because she had several of her own she was looking forward to sharing.

After returning to the hotel, Gage called his contact once again from the temperamental pay phone in the lobby. Although it took three tries, he was finally able to get through to the office in Athens.

"There's been a slight problem," he reported to Blythe, who was counting out drachmas for the brightly colored postcards she'd selected from a rack on the registration counter.

Blythe slipped the postcards into her purse, along with her change. "Why am I not surprised? I suppose she's on her way to some other island?"

"No, she's still on her way here. But they got a late start. The last report has the yacht scheduled to arrive sometime after midnight."

"Oh." As much as she wanted desperately to talk with Natasha, Blythe was disappointed that the woman's untimely arrival would interfere with their plans.

"You know," Gage suggested mildly, "Natasha has to be in her eighties. Even as lively as she admittedly seems to be for her age, the lady undoubtedly needs her beauty sleep."

"That's probably the case," Blythe agreed quickly.

"And, since we've waited this long, I suppose morning would be soon enough to interview her."

"She'd be fresher," Blythe said, getting into the spirit of the conversation. "So, her memory would undoubtedly be better."

"Makes sense to me," Gage said, pleased they were able to settle things so easily. He glanced down at his watch. "In the meantime, I've got some things to take care of. Will you be okay by yourself?"

"I'll be fine." More than fine, Blythe considered. Because she'd be preparing for what she knew was going to be the most important night of her life.

"Terrific." He kissed her, a brief kiss that ended too soon and left behind a flare of heat. "I'll be at your door at nine on the dot."

"I'll be waiting," Blythe promised. "With bells on."

He appeared to consider that for a moment. "Not bad," he decided. "While not exactly the fantasy I had in mind, it definitely has possibilities."

His grin warmed her all the way to her toes. He walked her across the courtyard, to her arched blue door, where he kissed her one last time. This kiss was longer. And hotter. And tested his resolve more than any thus far today.

Reminding himself again that he'd always been known for his patience, Gage reluctantly broke the heated contact, even as he wondered idly when he'd become such a masochist.

As she waited for evening, Blythe felt like Maggie the Cat, stuck on that hot tin roof. Finally, unable to remain alone in her hotel room any longer, she decided to walk down to the docks and buy some flowers she'd seen for sale in one of the stalls. And some candles, she considered, as she glanced around the room. Tonight was going to be a very special night. She wanted to set a lushly romantic mood.

Not that it would be difficult, she assured herself as she walked back up the hill forty-five minutes later, shopping bags in hand. The island was tailor-made for romance.

A tangy salt breeze perfumed with flowers ruffled her hair and the Mediterranean sun shone warm on her face. Despite her eagerness to talk with Natasha, Blythe couldn't remember ever feeling happier.

She heard a car engine behind her and turned, thinking—hoping—that it might be Gage. The welcoming smile faded from her lips as she realized the battered pickup truck loaded with produce was definitely not their rental jeep. The driver shouldn't be pushing the engine so hard, she thought, listening to the protesting rattle of the motor. The hill was steep and the truck was old.

She moved over to the side of the narrow, twisting road as far as she could, giving the driver room to pass. When the strident blast of a car horn pierced the perfumed air, she glanced back over her shoulder.

It was then she realized, with an icy flash of awareness, that the truck was headed straight toward her.

As he drove back to the hotel, Gage's mind was, admittedly, not on the case. Instead he was thinking about Blythe. And the romantic evening he'd just completed

arranging. Caught up in a silken web of sensual fantasies, he was only vaguely aware of the ancient produce
truck in front of him.

Old instincts, however, died hard and he did notice on
some subconscious level that the truck, which was being eaten alive by rust, had no license plate. Which, he
supposed, probably wasn't all that unusual for a farm
truck here on the island. The muffler was shot and dragging on the ground, which, given the age and condition
of the truck, also wasn't a surprise.

What didn't fit was the fact that the truck seemed to
be going too fast for the dangerous driving conditions.

It disappeared around a tight corner. A moment later,
Gage followed.

It was then his heart stopped in his throat.

He saw Blythe, strolling up the road. With the truck
headed straight toward her. He laid on the horn and
punched the gas pedal to the floor. Time took on a slow-
motion feel as he was forced to watch the murderous
events unfold.

For a fleeting instant that seemed to last an eternity,
Blythe stood frozen to the spot, unable to move. Unable
to breathe. When the blast of the jeep horn shook her
from her fear-induced paralysis, she dropped her shopping bags, turned and began desperately scrambling up
the rocky cliff. It was either that or over the side.

Her heart was threatening to burst out of her chest.
When a rock she'd grabbed hold of broke free, she nearly
fell directly into the path of the truck which was loom-
ing even closer. Just in time, her fingers closed around an
outcropping of stone and she managed, just barely, to
hang on as the bumper of the truck whizzed past her legs.

There was the grating scrape of metal against rock.
Then the roar of the engine as the truck continued on up

the hill, followed by the ear-piercing screech of brakes as Gage pulled the jeep to a shuddering stop. He was out of the driver's seat like a rocket.

"Are you all right?"

Although she couldn't hear his words over the cacophonous pounding of her heart in her ears, she could see the tortured fear on his face. In his eyes.

"I'm fine." She clung to him, her voice shaky, but amazingly strong, considering the circumstances.

"We're taking you to a doctor."

"That's not necessary." She let go of him long enough to attempt to stand on her own and belatedly discovered her little show of independence was a mistake.

"That's it," Gage said as he scooped her into his arms and carried her back to the jeep. "This is one case where you don't get a vote, Boss Lady."

"I TOLD YOU I was fine," Blythe told Gage when they were alone again in her room after the brief examination.

"It never hurts to check." He was sitting beside her on the mattress and frowned at the bruise darkening her cheekbone. A cold, killing rage rose inside him as he considered how close he'd come to losing her. "Perhaps we should stay in tonight."

The scenario was admittedly attractive. But there was something else to consider. "You may be in danger." There, he'd said it out loud.

"Nonsense." Leaning forward, she pressed a silky kiss against his scowling lips. "I'm not going to be frightened of some rustic farmer who's never learned how to drive."

"What if he wasn't a farmer?"

He watched the shadow move across her eyes and realized that she'd considered that very same thing herself. "If he wasn't," she said simply, "you'll protect me."

"I'm damn well going to try." He pulled her against him and kissed her with hot and desperate passion.

"Damn!" she complained when the long kiss finally ended.

"What?"

She held out her hand. "I broke a nail."

Although there was nothing remotely funny about what had happened, what had almost happened, Gage threw back his head and laughed.

THE RESTAURANT, a small, simple taverna, was perched like a bird's nest overlooking the sea. Their waiter, a huge man with muttonchop sideburns and a curled mustache led them to their table, situated on an outdoor balcony.

"This is incredible," she said, after the waiter, who'd introduced himself as Stavros, had seated them, lit the candle in the hurricane glass, then left them with a carafe of wine he'd drawn straight from a nearby barrel.

"It's not bad."

Gage looked enormously pleased with himself. And no wonder, Blythe thought. She couldn't have imagined a more unabashedly romantic spot to begin their fantasy night than dining beneath the stars, to the sound of the waves. "Is this another of Connor's suggestions?"

"Actually, I found it all by myself."

"But how? I thought you said you'd never been to Greece."

"I haven't. But I am a detective," he reminded her with a grin. "So, I just did a little detecting, and here we are."

"You really are incredible."

Talk about incredible! She was wearing a strapless white dress that revealed a weakening view of her voluptuous breasts, while the full, floaty skirt showed off her long legs. Her perfumed flesh gleamed golden in the flickering glow of the candlelight.

"I just hope you still think so in the morning."

It was her turn to smile. "Oh, I have a feeling you needn't have any worries in that regard, Gage."

He reached across the table and touched his fingers to the side of her face. "If that turns out to be the case, it's because of you. Because of the way you make me feel."

His touch, the warmth of his gaze, made Blythe glad she was already sitting down. "Flatterer," she said softly.

"It's the truth."

His expression turned immeasurably solemn. Blythe dipped her head to conceal her own turmoiled emotions.

How was it that he could say things that coming from any other man would seem like some polished script, but from Gage were obviously the truth? Perhaps, Blythe mused, because the flattering words only echoed her own feelings.

She'd never felt about another man the way she'd felt about Gage Remington from the beginning. And, she knew, she never would.

Following the Hellenic paradox that the simpler the restaurant, the better the food, they began the meal with daffodil yellow zucchini blossoms stuffed with rice, bits of ripe, red tomatoes and oregano that proved to be every bit as delicious as they were pretty.

Bowls of salad, lumpy with feta cheese and black olives, were followed by the main course—moussaka for Blythe, and chicken cooked in cinnamon-and-tomato sauce for Gage.

"No, no. You are eating it all wrong," Stavros scolded as he paused by their table long enough to refill their wineglasses. He literally plucked Gage's fork from his fingers. "Women and chicken should both be picked up in the hands."

The proclamation, pronounced as if he were an oracle handing down instructions atop Mt. Delphi, made Gage laugh and Blythe blush.

As she watched him take a bite out of a sauce-laden drumstick, she was struck with a sudden feeling of déjà vu.

"I can't believe you've never gone on an old-fashioned American picnic." Patrick plucked a piece of fried chicken from the wicker basket. They were at his ranch in Wyoming, sitting on an Indian blanket in a field of colorful blue and yellow wildflowers.

"I told you I've been deprived," Alexandra complained prettily. She watched his strong white teeth bite into the drumstick, remembered how those same teeth had thrilled her last night, nipping at the tender flesh at the inside of her thighs, and felt a surge of desire so strong it rocked her.

"Poor baby." Reading the hunger of another kind rising in her expressive dark eyes, he tossed the chicken aside and lowered her onto the blanket. "How can I ever make it up to you?"

She twined her arms around his neck. "This is," she sighed blissfully as he began unbuttoning her sleeveless denim blouse, "a very good beginning."

"Blythe?" Gage lowered the chicken leg to the plate. She'd suddenly gone as white as the tablecloth. She was staring at him as if she'd seen a ghost. "What's wrong?"

Shaken by the image that had seemed so amazingly real, Blythe struggled to return her mind to the present. Which was difficult to do when, as impossible as it seemed, she could still feel Patrick Reardon's wide dark hands cupping her breasts. His harshly cut lips closing around an excruciatingly sensitive nipple.

"I don't know."

Her dark eyes were wide and unfocused. Her hand, as he covered it with his, was ice cold. "Are you sick?" He glanced around, wanting the check so they could leave. Now.

"No." She shook her head, then gave herself another stiff mental shake. "I'm all right." Her vision cleared and she viewed the unmasked concern—make that fear—on his rugged face. "Really."

The color was returning to her cheeks. Her hand, beneath his on the tablecloth, warmed. Whatever had been wrong had passed, Gage determined.

"Was it something I said? Or did? The food?"

"No."

How could she explain that she'd felt as if she'd suddenly been removed from the present and whisked back in time? How could she tell him that of all the dreams she'd had about Alexandra and Patrick these past months, this one—occurring while she was fully awake—had been the most vivid yet? How did she reveal that she'd been imagining making love to one man—who'd been dead for more than sixty years—while anticipating making love to another?

"I was just thinking about Alexandra and Patrick," she hedged.

"That's not so surprising." The couple had continued to infiltrate his mind as well, ever since Blythe had hired him to investigate the long-ago marriage. And murder.

"Did your investigation reveal whether or not they'd ever taken a trip to Wyoming?"

"Actually, they did. For their six-month anniversary," Gage revealed. "Alexandra wanted to see Patrick's ranch."

That explained it, Blythe thought with a rush of cooling relief. Falling under the spell of the stars, the romantic mood, and the man, she'd blended the story of their trip to Wyoming with her own feelings for Gage.

"I was going to tell you before we left to come here," he said. "But I found you drinking that champagne, and we got sidetracked. Then you spent most of the various flights from L.A. to Greece sleeping.

"Then, selfishly having my own plans for tonight, I figured, since it wasn't exactly an earth-shattering revelation, it could wait until tomorrow."

Somehow, Blythe wasn't as surprised as she might have been. After all, in a way this had happened before, when she'd been in Hawaii with Alan, and had fantasized about making love to Gage in that hot spring in Colorado. Afterwards, she'd learned the location was where Alexandra and Patrick had spent their honeymoon.

"So I couldn't have known."

"Not from me." He gave her a long look. Then he paused, as if carefully choosing his words. "But that doesn't mean much. Not where those two are concerned."

"Are you saying—"

"I haven't exactly experienced whatever flash you obviously just had. But I have had some incredibly realistic dreams that can't be explained away by logic."

She was dying to ask him if, during these dreams, he was a distant observer. Or, if like in her case, he felt as if the action was actually happening to him. Although it made absolutely no more sense than anything else that had been happening lately, Blythe felt strangely guilty about fantasizing about Patrick. Especially when Gage had gone to so much trouble to set the scene for a romantic evening.

"This is our night," she decided. "Why don't we agree to a moratorium on Patrick and Alexandra?"

"You're on." Even as he agreed, Gage had the nagging feeling that keeping thoughts of the star-crossed pair at bay was going to be a helluva lot easier said than done.

6

THE SEA, turquoise in the dazzling Greek sunshine,
turned to jet at night. Overhead, stars glittered like diamonds strewn over a black velvet sky; a full white
moon cast a liquid silver path on the water.

"I almost expect to see Poseidon," Blythe said as she
and Gage walked along the waterfront after dinner.

"Riding his chariot across the waves, trident raised
toward the moon," he agreed. His arm tightened around
her waist as he looked down at her, enjoying the way the
shimmering moonlight played across her exquisite face.
"And the instant he saw you, standing here beside the sea,
his marriage to Amphitrite would be history. Because,
being a very clever, not to mention incredibly virile god,
he'd recognize what I already know . . . that not even a
goddess could hold a candle to a siren like you."

Once again, the clever words, designed for seduction,
could have been coined by a Hollywood scriptwriter. But
Blythe knew they came from the heart. Which was why
they had such a devastating effect on her.

As she allowed him to draw her into the circle of his
arms, Blythe tried to convince herself that it was the
moonlight that had her feeling so bewitched, that it was
the wine that she'd drunk with dinner that had her feeling so bewildered.

But she knew, with ever fiber of her being, that it was
neither the moonlight nor the wine. It was Gage.

She lifted her hands to his shoulders. Her eyes were wide and solemn as they met his steady, watchful gaze. "I don't need the words." Not with him. Never with him.

"Too bad." Smiling a little, he drew her against him. "Because I suddenly have the need to say them."

Their bodies were close. She could feel his heartbeat—steady, but strong—against her own escalating one. "I've never met a man like you," she mused, half to herself, half to Gage. "Most men, especially in Hollywood, are always playing games. But you don't."

Her scent surrounded him, as sultry and exotic as the image she portrayed on the screen. The first time he'd seen her, striding toward him on those long gorgeous legs, he'd mistakenly dismissed her as just another egocentric, air-headed actress. For a man who'd always prided himself on his ability to make snap judgments about people—there'd been more than one instance when his life had depended on it—Gage had never been so far off base.

"I've never enjoyed playing games." In the distance, music was playing, drifting on the warm sea breeze. Loosing track of their surroundings, as so often happened when he was with Blythe, he began absently swaying to the rhythm. "Probably because I've never been very good at them." The night breeze, perfumed with the scent of sun-drenched flowers, ruffled her hair. When he smoothed a few errant strands away from her face, then kissed a heretofore undiscovered sensual place behind her ear, Blythe felt her blood begin to hum again.

"I think," she murmured as she tilted her head back, giving him access to her neck, "that there are some games you're very, very good at."

Her skin glowed in the moonlight like pearls. He ran his lips down her throat. "I'm not playing any games, Blythe." Across her bare shoulders. "Not tonight."

She was trembling. But not because she was chilled. Her silken flesh beneath his mouth was warm from the fever flowing in her blood.

"I want you." His voice was harsh, aroused. In the moonlight, his eyes glittered with a fierce, primal hunger that brought to mind the ancient, savage gods that had once ruled these lands. He fisted his hand in her hair, tilting her head back. "So much I ache with it."

Desire, and something much stronger, much deeper, had etched harsh lines into his rugged face. Knowing that they were standing on the brink of something far more important than a mere night of shared sexual pleasure, Blythe paused, wanting to choose her words carefully.

And in that slight hesitation, the sensual moment was lost as their strip of beach was suddenly filled with a vast promenade of dancers and musicians.

"What the hell?" Gage's blistering gaze was a very long way from amusement.

"Oh, it's a wedding party," Blythe said, recognizing the couple surrounded by the laughing, singing throng. When she'd been on location on Crete, the director had incorporated a similar scene in the lighthearted teenage romance film. But this one was all the more pleasurable, because it was real.

"They've got lousy timing," he muttered.

"Don't be a spoilsport. You're the one who wanted a romantic night," she reminded him teasingly. "What could be more romantic than a wedding?"

Before Gage could respond, Blythe was dragged away, caught up in the procession of merrymakers. Reaching out, she caught hold of Gage's hand and brought him along with her.

Knowing when he was licked, Gage gave in.

The procession, dancing to the music of the mandolins and zithers, wound through the narrow streets, back up the rocky hillside, to the same taverna where Gage and Blythe had finished eating dinner. As Stavros greeted the bride and groom with effusive kisses, a relative who spoke English explained to Blythe and Gage that their waiter was a third cousin on the groom's mother's side.

It appeared the entire town had turned out for the reception. Wine flowed, toasts were made. One by one the guests wished blessings on the newly married couple. Then, when everyone fell suddenly silent, Blythe noticed that they were looking at Gage and her.

"It's our turn," she said.

"The only toasts I know are from my old fraternity days," he muttered. "And believe me, they're not suitable for mixed company. Let alone a wedding."

"Don't worry. I think I can remember what to say." Lacing their fingers together, she approached the happy pair.

"Kala Stefana," she said to the beautiful, dark-haired bride. Gage, having no idea what she'd said, smiled at the bride and shook the groom's hand.

The obviously pleased bride answered in a rush of rapid-fire Greek. Several nearby volunteer translators told Blythe that she'd been recognized and that both families considered it an honor that the famous movie actress would deign to be a guest at their celebration.

Smiling broadly, the bride's mother, dressed in a flowing rainbow hued dress, stepped forward. *"Ghia sas!* Welcome!" she said as she gave both Blythe and Gage handful of *kouferta*—the sugar almonds traditionally used as favors at Greek weddings.

Now that she'd been recognized, Blythe knew that to leave early might insult the family and bring a pall on the celebration. So, though she longed to be alone with Gage, she agreed to stay for the dancing. Which, it appeared, seemed destined to last all night.

Finally, nearly two hours later, they were able to slip away unnoticed.

"Well, that was certainly a night to remember," Gage said, as they strolled back to the hotel through the dark and quiet streets, the music fading in the distance.

"I hope you didn't mind," she answered. "But, once they recognized me—"

"I know." He gave her a reassuring smile that flashed a brilliant white in the moonlight. "Don't worry, Blythe. I don't have any trouble playing second fiddle to a world famous star."

"Alan did." The words were out of her mouth before Blythe could censor them.

She was relieved when Gage didn't appear disturbed by the intrusion of her former fiancé's name. "Sturgess is a damn fool," he said with a shrug. "Along with being a jerk and a lying cheat with the morals of an alley cat.

"But, to get back to the original topic, I'm not going to deny that I hadn't had other plans for tonight. I mean, when I mentioned dancing beneath the stars, I sure as hell didn't expect my partner to have a mustache."

"I thought you did very well," Blythe said, grinning at the memory of Gage being coaxed into the circle of traditional male dancers.

"Ah, but you're prejudiced."

"Probably. But you were still the best-looking man there. And nearly the best dancer."

It was a blatant exaggeration. But one Gage was se-cretly enjoying too much to contradict. "Lord, you are good for a man's ego. And to tell you the truth, I ended up having a pretty good time."

"It was fun, wasn't it?" Blythe smiled as she thought about how different the celebration had seemed from her own disrupted marriage to Alan.

"As much fun as it could be, without throwing in an earthquake," he agreed, revealing that they were on the same wavelength again. They'd reached their small, in-timate hilltop hotel. "By the way, I kept meaning to ask, what did you say to the bride?"

"Oh. Good crowning." Although she exercised regu-larly, Blythe was a little out of breath. It had not been easy, climbing the steep hills in high heels. "It's a tradi-tional Greek wedding wish."

"What did she say to you?"

Suddenly, unreasonably, self-conscious, Blythe pre-tended an intense interest in the angel that had been painted in the carved niche over the arched turquoise door. "I'm not sure."

"You know," Gage said mildly, "for such a famous, hotshot actress, you're a rotten liar, sweetheart."

"You have to understand, in this country, marriage traditions are as full of ritual response as a Greek Ortho-dox mass."

"What did she say, Blythe?"

He'd pulled out his calm, patient interrogation tactics again. It was all Blythe could do not to squirm beneath the steady stare. She wished she hadn't hedged in the first place. Because by doing so, she'd given the traditional phrase much more meaning that if she'd just told Gage outright.

Buying time, she dug around in her satin bag for the hotel key.

"Blythe?"

"All right!" No wonder he was so good at what he did. She couldn't imagine him letting anyone off the hook. Not even her. *Especially* her. "Loosely translated, she wished the same to me. At my own wedding."

He considered that for a minute. The idea, Gage decided with some surprise, definitely had merit. "Nice tradition. I think we ought to give it some thought."

Before his words could sink in, he put his arm around her shoulder and looked up at the bright sky. "Would you just look at all those stars."

Blythe's mind was whirling as she tried to decide whether or not he'd actually just suggested marriage. "What did you just say?"

"I was pointing out the stars. There's the North Star. And the Big Dipper."

"Before that."

He ignored her. "And Orion.... Do you remember the story of Dionysus and Ariadne?"

Frustrated by his seeming change of subject, but not wanting to embarrass herself by pressing Gage further, when she'd undoubtedly misunderstood what he'd meant only as a casual comment, Blythe thought back to the long-ago mythology class she'd taken her freshman year of college.

"Wasn't Ariadne the daughter of Minos, king of Crete?"

"That's her." Gage rewarded her with a smile that reminded her of the gold stars her tutors on movie sets used to stick on her spelling papers. "She fell in love with Theseus when he went to Crete to slay the Minotaur."

"She gave him a ball of jeweled thread, so he could find his way out of the labyrinth," Blythe remembered. "Then, after he killed the Minotaur, Theseus left Crete and took Ariadne with him. But didn't he desert her on some other island?"

"Naxos," Gage confirmed. "Which is where Dionysus found her."

"Was that before or after drinking with his satyr buddies and fooling around with all those naked nymphs?"

"Hey, the guy may have admittedly been a bit of a playboy, but he knew a good woman when he spotted one. Anyway, he married Ariadne, which, needless to say, relieved her father immensely, seeing how, having been so publicly dumped by Theseus, her marriage marketability had dropped slightly."

Blythe scowled. "She was lucky to have found out about Theseus before she'd made the mistake and married the wrong man."

"My thoughts exactly." Gage decided there was no need to point out the parallels in their situation. "And then, to prove how much he loved her, after Ariadne died, Dionysus made the constellation Corona Borealis out of her bridal wreath."

"Making her immortal," Blythe murmured.

"Part blessing, part curse. Talk about your good news, bad news scenarios."

"Wouldn't you want to live forever?"

Gage considered that for a moment. "I suppose," he said, in that slow, thoughtful way she'd come to respect and admire, "that it would depend a lot on who I was living with."

His eyes glittering in the streaming silver moonlight, he drew her back against him. The fluttering he was always able to instill in her heart increased.

He took both her hands and lifted them to his lips. "What I said earlier, about wanting you . . . I meant it, Blythe."

She felt a surge of excitement mixed with a tingling of fear. He looked so serious. "I want you, too," she whispered on lips that had gone suddenly, painfully dry.

His lips curved. Just a little. "I know." He drew in a deep breath, then let it out. Gage couldn't remember ever feeling so tense. Not even the time he and Cait had run into that dark alley after a trio of gangbangers who'd just pulled off a drive-by shooting.

"I really do want you," she repeated. "But it's important that you understand that I've never been into casual sex." Blythe wanted him to know that what was to happen was special. Unique.

"Believe me, sweetheart, there's nothing casual about how I feel. In fact, the truth is, I've never needed a woman like I need you." His deceptively mild tone was a riveting contrast to the passion blazing in his eyes. "And I'm not sure how to handle that."

His unrelenting honesty was only one of the many reasons she'd fallen in love with him. *Love.* The word reeled in her head. It was a word they'd both been avoiding, even as it had continued to grow between them, larger and more undeniable.

There would be plenty of time for talking, Blythe decided. For now, she was willing to bask in the warm glow of her realization. At this moment, all she wanted was to satisfy this curiosity, this desire, that had been ripping away at her self-control since the moment she'd met him.

"I'd say that you're doing pretty good." Her smile was one of sensual invitation. "So far."

She watched the tension literally slide off his shoulders. His grin could have kept her warm in an Antarctic blizzard. "And the night's still young."

He took the antique brass key from her hand and unlocked the door.

The room was small, but cozy. The walls were whitewashed, the window shutters, like the door, had been painted turquoise. The focal point of the room was the bed, which had been built into an alcove.

The room carried her scent. It surrounded him, enveloped him, drew him into the mists. As he stood beside the bed, looking down at Blythe, drinking in her incredible beauty a hundred—a thousand—different feelings were fighting for control inside him.

"You are so beautiful." He shook his head in awe that of all the men in the world, Blythe had, for some reason he knew better than to analyze, chosen him. He combed his fingers through her breeze-tousled hair. The dark waves felt like silk and smelled like temptation. "Sometimes—like now—when you look at me that way, with your heart shining in those magnificent gypsy eyes, I don't know what to say."

"I told you." She lifted her hands to frame his unsmiling face between her palms. "You don't have to say anything, Gage. I don't need the words. Not from you." Her gaze was warm and earnest. Her lips, like her hands, trembled ever so slightly. "Never from you."

Breathing out a deep, relieved sigh, he lowered his forehead to hers. "I've wanted to be like this with you from almost the moment I first saw you."

"I know." If she lived a thousand lifetimes, she'd never forget the instant when, at his rough command, she'd yanked off her sunglasses and felt a jolt of something that impossibly felt like recognition. "Because I've felt the same way."

"It was like someone had hit me with a sledgehammer." Feeling unreasonably clumsy, Gage skimmed his hands down her sides, where they settled at her hips.

His strong, possessive touch felt like a brand, threatening to burn its way through the filmy white silk. "For me it was as if a bolt of lightning had suddenly struck out of the clear blue sky." She drew in a quick, shuddering breath as he bent closer. "It was too much. Too fast."

"No." His mouth touched hers. Once, twice, a third time. Her lips were soft as snowflakes, as potent as whiskey. "It wasn't nearly enough."

Gage knew that he'd never get enough of her. Fighting back his own pounding needs, he caught her bottom lip between his teeth, then, when he felt her long, drawn out sigh, soothed the fullness with his tongue.

"I was afraid," she admitted.

"Of me?" The revelation was not a pleasant one.

"No." Her lips plucked reassuringly at his. "Never of you." She pressed her body against his. "I was afraid I'd go crazy." He felt so strong. So solid. So right. "Crazy for wanting this." When his lips skimmed along her jawline, she thrust her hands through his thick dark hair and dragged his mouth back to his. "Crazy for wanting you."

His blood was pounding thickly in his head, in his loins. God help him, he'd tried. Gage had wanted to take things slow, vowed to be gentle. But he'd waited too long and his need was too strong. And he hadn't planned on her hot, avid mouth driving him beyond tenderness into madness. She could have been an ancient siren, luring him with her temptress song into dark, dangerous waters.

Half-crazed himself, desperate to touch her, he yanked down the back zipper of her strapless dress, causing it to fall into a white silk pool at her feet.

Blythe closed her eyes and swayed, moaning raggedly when he took her breasts in his greedy hands, warming them, molding them. He'd been starving for her for too long; having finally abandoned abstinence, he intended to feast. He was merciless, tasting her silken flesh with his lips, his tongue, his teeth.

Desire. Passion. Excitement. He tasted it on her slick, hot flesh, felt it in the way her fingers dug painfully into his shoulders, heard it in her shimmering sighs and ragged moans. He savored each new sensation he brought to her, drinking in the sensual sight of the riot of emotions that swept across her face and clouded her eyes.

Needing more, he slipped his fingers beneath the ivory lace cut low on her hips. His touch was as wicked as it was practiced, drawing a faint moan from between her parted lips as he traced his fingers through the nest of sable curls.

No less eager to touch him as he was touching her, needing to torment him as he was tormenting her, aching for the feel of flesh against flesh, Blythe yanked Gage's white shirt open. Buttons skittered across the floor, ignored. She arched against him, fitting her soft feminine curves to his hard warrior's body.

On a half groan, half curse, he dragged her down onto the mattress, where they sank deeply into the thick goose down. His mouth captured her, seduced her, drew her deeper and deeper into the mists.

He stripped away her silk panties, exposing her to his heated gaze. Her creamy skin glowed like pearls; a rosy flush, like poppies, bloomed across her chest. Her hair was a thick sable cloud over her shoulders, her eyes were wide and as dark as obsidian.

"I've dreamed of you like this." He lay beside her, drinking in the sight of her, lying in the moonlight streaming in through the open shutters.

She wanted to tell him that she'd dreamed of him, too. But when he began blazing a path down first her throat, then her torso with hot, wet, openmouthed kisses, she could no longer talk. She could barely breath. All she could manage were throaty moans and shuddering breaths.

Greedily, his mouth returned to her breasts. When his lips closed around a taut nipple and tugged, Blythe felt a series of tiny explosions that rippled their way down from her breast to the source of heat pooling between her legs. When he took the other pebbled bud between his finger and thumb, she moaned and arched her back.

Gage explored every inch of her alluring body with his hands and found her wonderful. He tasted every bit of fragrant flesh and knew that there had never been— would never be—a woman more perfectly suited to him than this one.

With a hunger that equaled his own, she began tugging at his slacks, but he deftly avoided her, shifting away from her seeking hands. Although he'd always prided himself on his control, had always considered himself a considerate lover, Gage knew that if he allowed those questing fingers to so much as skim against his throbbing sex, he'd have no choice but to take her quickly.

And he wasn't ready. Not by a long shot.

Her body was sleek, moist, responsive. She'd abandoned inhibitions, surrendered control, trusting him implicitly. His name tumbled from between her lips as he laid a wet swathe down her stomach with his tongue. Her hands thrust into his hair, urging his head lower.

Gage willingly obliged.

His teeth scraped against her inner thighs, drawing a moan from deep in her throat. He took hold of her hips, lifted her to his mouth and feasted.

His tongue dove into the hot center of her pleasure. Blythe cried out as the first orgasm shuddered through her, but before she could recover, he was driving her up again, higher and higher, to peak after torturous peak. He watched, incredibly aroused by her abandonment. She was hot and damp and exhausted. But still she wanted more.

"Please." She writhed on the tangled sheets, fusing her body to his, struggling to capture him between her legs. It was not a plea, but a demand. "I want you, Gage. Now."

He left her only long enough to strip off the last barricade between them and to sheathe himself. The idea that he'd think to protect her at a time like this told Blythe once again that she'd chosen well. But then he was kneeling between her quivering thighs, looking down at her with such a savage intensity it took her breath away.

"You're mine." He lowered his body against hers. Torso to torso, thighs to thighs.

"Yours," she whispered.

His eyes locked on hers. Watching. Waiting. "Forever."

She could not speak. But her lips, unbearably dry, formed the word, *yes.* With his eyes still open, still on hers, he plunged into her, with one strong, deep stroke. Her body arched, absorbing the sudden surge of male strength. He saw her stunned pleasure, experienced a surge of satisfaction that he'd been the one to put it there.

But then she locked her long legs around his hips and he felt her muscles close around him like a tight, moist velvet fist. And Gage was lost.

Burying his face in her hair, wallowing in its fragrance, he allowed his body to take over. He drove into her welcoming warmth, harder and harder, deeper and deeper, matching the upward thrust of her hips, claiming her in a frenzy of power and speed.

Blythe cried out his name again as he poured himself into her, as he called out hers. He felt her climax, like an explosion around him. The aftershocks seemed to go on forever.

Sprawled on top of her, too spent to move, Gage tried to draw lifesaving breath into his burning lungs. And even as he tried to tell himself that it had never been like this before, somewhere, in the far reaches of his mind, a distant voice insisted that wasn't honestly the case.

"I've dreamed about this," Blythe said quietly. Her hands were no longer clutching at his bare back, but caressing his scratched and wounded flesh in long, slow strokes. "So many times."

He lifted his head. "About you and me?"

"Sometimes." Her expressive eyes were home to an appealing blend of warmth and confusion. "But at other times—"

"It's them." Gage swore quietly. He rolled off her, but unwilling to let go of her quite yet, he lay on his side and put his arms around her. "Patrick and Alexandra."

Blythe sighed. "Do you believe in past lives?"

Having always considered himself a practical, feet-on-the-ground kind of guy, he immediately answered, "No."

"Neither did I." She lifted her gaze to his. "But lately, I can't help wondering."

"It's because we've both been obsessing on them," Gage insisted. "Mix that in with the chemistry that has flared between us from the beginning, and it was probably inevitable that we'd end up blending their stories in with our fantasies."

"I suppose you're right." Her expression, and her tone revealed that as much as she wanted to believe Gage's explanation, she wasn't entirely convinced.

"It's the only plausible answer," Gage insisted.

Not wanting to get into an argument, so soon after having experienced the most exciting, fulfilling lovemaking of her life, Blythe didn't answer. Instead, she snuggled closer and pressed her lips against his chest.

Gage ran his hand down her hair. "I don't think I'll ever get enough of you."

She tilted her head back and smiled up at him. "Good. Because I don't intend to let you."

Then, twining her arms around his neck, she lifted her mouth to his.

Outside the open window, leaves from the olive trees whispered, adding harmony to the plaintive, sad sound of a mandolin drifting on the soft Mediterranean sea breeze.

Inside, Gage and Blythe took turns pleasuring one another. Now that the initial fiery flare of passion had burned itself out, the pace blissfully mellowed. Their slow kisses turned dreamy as their hands moved lingeringly over warming flesh.

And this time, as they floated back to earth, entwined in each other's arms, Blythe felt a contentment so rich, so sweet, it brought tears to her eyes.

7

THE TOWN WAS QUIET and pink in the early morning light as Gage and Blythe drove through the deserted streets. The houses were cool and shuttered, the still air was drenched with the sweet, lingering perfume of night flowering stock and jasmine.

Blythe drank in the sights, the scents. "I don't believe I've ever been happier," she murmured.

Gage braked for a herd of the seemingly ubiquitous goats being herded through the narrow, winding roadway. The tiny copper bells around the goats' necks added a tinkling accompaniment to the tolling of church bells.

"There's still a chance that Natasha won't be able to tell us anything helpful." Knowing how much the project meant to Blythe, he hated thinking that they'd gone to so much trouble, traveled so far, only to have the former makeup artist turn out to be a dead end.

She heard the warning in his tone. And the concern. And, most of all the love. Blythe reached across the space between the two seats and placed her hand on his leg. "I know. But, believe it or not, I wasn't thinking about Natasha."

Her heart was in her eyes. "I was talking about us. How you made me feel last night. How I feel this morning." She swallowed as she chose her words carefully, wanting him to understand that what had happened last night was more than the result of a romantic, moon-spangled night. "I love you."

Gage let out a long breath. He had not realized exactly how badly he'd needed to hear those long awaited words. Giving thanks to whatever fates or ancient gods had brought them to this place, he covered her hand with his and asked, "When?"

"Did I realize how I felt?" A whispery gust of sea breeze fanned her hair. Blythe blew some errant strands from her eyes. "For certain last night." Her thoughtful gaze turned sober. "But to tell you the truth, I think I've loved you forever."

No poet could have penned such sweet words. No mortal playwright or novelist could have written a scene that made his heart soar so high. Or made him feel so humble.

With a groan of pleasure, he dragged her from her seat onto his lap, cupped the back of her neck, and covered her mouth with his.

"Oh, by the way," he said when the long satisfying kiss finally ended, "in case I've neglected mentioning it, I love you, too." His smiling lips plucked at hers. "So, when do you want to do it?"

She was slowly sinking under the sensual spell his lips were weaving. Even after all they'd shared last night, desire began to rise, sharp and sweet at the same time. She pressed her palm against his chest, felt the thunder of his heart and knew he was no less affected. "Do what?"

Threading his hands through her thick hair, he pushed it away from her face. Lord, she was beautiful! Inside and out. And she was all his. Forever. He lowered his mouth to hers again and murmured, "Get married, of course."

"Married?"

Gage felt the change immediately. An involuntary stiffening of her spine, a tensing of her lips beneath his. Warning himself not to ruin things by going off half-cocked, he slowly lifted his head. "When two people love one another, it's usually customary," he said with a casualness he was a very long way from feeling. "Even in Hollywood."

Blythe knew she should not be surprised. If she'd been honest with herself, she would have admitted that although he'd waited until now to tell her he loved her, over these past months she'd sensed that his feelings went deeper than a mere detective-client relationship.

"Three days ago I was engaged to Alan."

"And now you're not." His tone was mild but his eyes were not. Realizing that Gage was not a man to share his emotions easily, Blythe knew that if she wasn't extremely careful, she could end up ruining what they had together.

When she would have slid back over to her own seat, his arms tightened around her. "Unless I'm mistaken, you just told me you loved me."

"I did, but—"

"And I love you," he continued, cutting her off. He was angry, Gage realized with surprise. Really angry, bordering on furious. It was unlike him to come so close to losing his temper. "So, I'm having trouble understanding what the problem is, Blythe."

It was the intense calmness of his tone that was the tip-off. The quieter his voice, the more measured the words, the more dangerous the man was. Blythe wondered why she'd never realized that before. Wondered how many criminals had mistakenly underestimated his seemingly unrelenting patience. "I want to say yes," she began haltingly.

"Then say it."

He made it sound so easy. And perhaps, for him, it was. "What would people say?" The moment she said the words, she realized how ridiculous they sounded.

His oath was short and rude. "What the hell do you care?"

"I don't. Not really." That was the truth. "But don't you think it's awfully soon to begin making plans?"

"No."

There was, Blythe saw, no reasoning with him. "I hadn't realized you could be so hardheaded."

Gage was tempted to counter that he hadn't known she could be so damn stupid. "Now you do," he said instead.

She closed her eyes. Then opened them and tried again. "I already made one mistake, with Alan—"

"Are you comparing me to that stuffed-shirt bastard?"

"Of course not." She place a conciliatory hand on his arm and felt the muscle tense beneath her fingers. "Never."

He read the absolute truth in her distressed eyes. Heard it in her fervent tone.

"It's just that I need time. Time to figure out how to separate what I feel for you from what I've fantasized Alexandra feeling for Patrick." Her fingers tightened. "It won't change the fact that I love you. But right now, I'm just so confused. I need time to think."

"Anyone ever tell you that you think too damn much?"

"It sounds familiar." Cait and Lily had both urged her to trust her feelings where this man was concerned. Easier said than done, Blythe agonized now.

Her shoulders sagged. Watching her battling the moisture brimming in her eyes, Gage felt the war raging inside him. He didn't immediately respond to her ragged admission. By the time he felt capable of speaking calmly again, sympathy had won out over pride.

"All right. I won't push. Not now." He traced a finger around her trembling bottom lip. "Right now it's enough to know that you love me, Blythe." Her remarkable eyes were cautious. Almost fearful, making him realize that he had no choice but to give her time. And space. "But it won't be enough forever."

"I know." Her breath trembled out. She was on the verge of promising that she'd sort things out as soon as she could when a horn from a truck suddenly blared from behind them.

Gage swore, shifting into gear as Blythe quickly returned to her seat. "Timing, they say, is everything."

Blythe murmured a vague agreement to his muttered pronouncement, even as she silently thanked the burly driver for the propitious interruption.

Kyriako Papakosta was an immensely popular novelist, lionized in his home country. One look at the gleaming white yacht revealed equally strong foreign sales.

"Obviously restructuring ancient myths pays very well," Blythe murmured, recalling the last book the author had written, about a hero who'd reenacted Ulysses' travels.

"I've seen U.S. destroyers smaller than this ship," Gage agreed. "Looks as if Natasha has done all right for herself."

Her attention momentarily captured by the bright flags snapping in the morning breeze, Blythe murmured a vague agreement.

Natasha Kuryan proved a definite surprise. Although Blythe knew the petite woman had to be in her eighties, it was impossible to judge her age. She was dressed in vintage clothing reminiscent of a Russian Gypsy. Her snowy hair had been twisted into a long braid that hung over her shoulder and was tied with a piece of white lace.

"Welcome aboard." She greeted them with out-stretched hands. "I'm so sorry I've caused you so much difficulty. As I told your friend when he called yesterday from Athens on the ship-to-shore radio, your cables only caught up with us two days ago." She hadn't entirely lost her accent, even after all the years away from her home country. Her smile was quick and sincere, making her appear decades younger and giving a glimpse of the beauty she once had been.

"Time in the Greek isles," she told them needlessly, "does not necessarily move at the same speed as in the rest of the world."

"I've found that to be an advantage, at times," Gage answered, exchanging a warm, reminiscent glance with Blythe.

Never one to miss a thing, Natasha's bright green eyes sparkled with pleasure. Having been in love more times than she could count, she always enjoyed watching others experience similar pleasures.

"You're quite right," she agreed with a fond look up-ward, toward the bridge. A tall, muscular man, clad in jeans, a striped black-and-white fisherman's shirt, and blue billed cap waved at her. Natasha waved back.

"Kyriako has asked me to invite you to breakfast," she revealed. "He also will insist on giving you a tour of his pride and joy." Her beringed hand waved, encompass-ing the gleaming yacht.

"I'd like that," Blythe said. Gage immediately con-curred.

"It's really quite fascinating. He's turned it into a mu-seum."

"A museum of what?" Blythe asked.

"Of himself, of course." Natasha smiled with feminine indulgence. "Like most successful, handsome, Greek men, Kyriako is not lacking in ego."

She tilted her head, suddenly studying Gage as a diamond cutter might observe a newly mined stone. "You have Gary Cooper's profile," she decided, abruptly changing the subject. "Coop was so wonderfully handsome." She breathed a reminiscent sigh. "And such a marvelous lover."

Since neither Gage nor Blythe knew how to respond to such an intimate statement from a woman they'd just met, neither answered.

"Of course your eyes are pure Newman," she continued cataloguing Gage. "And although there's no real physical resemblance, you remind me a bit of Errol Flynn. With Gable's masculine sex appeal tossed in for good measure."

Gage grinned. "I'm flattered."

Natasha clapped her hands in obvious delight. "And you've got Gable's wonderfully wicked smile, too! A man with a smile like that can charm a woman into anything," she said to Blythe.

"So I've discovered," Blythe answered with a smile of her own.

"It's really too bad you didn't go into acting," Natasha told Gage. "You could have been a star."

"I prefer to leave the starring roles to Blythe."

"Well, that's not surprising. You know, my dear," she said, turning her attention to Blythe, "you are almost a dead ringer for Ava Gardner. In her younger years."

"I've been told that before," Blythe admitted.

"And no wonder." Natasha's gaze filled with admiration as it took a slow journey from the top of Blythe's head down to her feet, clad in ankle-tied espadrilles. "You don't see many hourglass figures anymore," she mused. "These days, everyone seems to be trying to starve themselves into those eating disorders clinics that have become all the rage."

"I've always had a healthy appetite." Blythe had long ago given up trying to buck nature by shaping her curvaceous body into popularly boyish lines.

"I can definitely attest to that," Gage agreed, his double entendre earning a quick, appreciative smile from Natasha and a faint blush from Blythe.

"Ava ate like a stevedore—fried chicken and hominy for breakfast, steak and milk shakes for lunch, and mountains of spaghetti for dinner," Natasha revealed. "But she never had any trouble meeting MGM's weekly weigh-ins. The other poor contract actresses continually deprived themselves, living on consommé and Mr. Mayer's famous lemon tea.

"I don't believe Ava ever drank tea. But she certainly drank everything else. In fact, she was the only woman I've ever seen who could smoke like a chimney, down brandy with champagne chasers and chew gum all at the same time. And still look glamorous doing it.

"Although even she couldn't stop the clock, she possessed a timeless beauty that even a lifetime of bad habits couldn't diminish."

Natasha's eyes turned thoughtful. And sad. "Alexandra was the same. She had the face, the bones, the *presence* that would have made her still stunning at ninety."

"Unfortunately, she didn't live to ninety," Blythe said quietly.

"No." The smile faded from the elderly woman's lips and eyes. "And that's why you've come. To talk about poor, tragic Alexandra."

"And Patrick," Blythe said.

"Yes." Natasha sighed. "It's a very long story. And a very sad one."

"That much we've figured out for ourselves," Gage said. "But since you did Alexandra's makeup while you were working at Xanadu, we were hoping you could clear up a few nagging gaps in the story."

She shook her white head and briefly closed her eyes. Blythe had the feeling that she'd mentally returned to the days when Hollywood stood for glamour and glitz. When stars were larger than life. And when one particular scandal rocked not only the movie community, but the world.

"Come into the sitting room," she said. "I've instructed the cook to make coffee and pastries. We can talk there."

Blythe and Gage followed her into a spacious cabin comfortably furnished in complimentary shades of blue, white and yellow. A pot of fragrant green basil had been placed on a nearby table, a twin of the one Blythe had seen on the deck outside.

She remembered reading from yesterday's guidebook that basil—also known as basiliko, the kingly one—was believed to be the plant St. Helena had found growing at the foot of the cross. Greek seamen used the plant as a talisman, to protect their ships.

Inviting them to sit on the white sofa, Natasha settled into the yellow-and-white awning striped chair on a swirl of lacy peasant skirts.

She took her time, pouring thick Greek coffee into small white cups, placing almond pastries onto plates, arranging damask napkins. Blythe had the feeling that she was buying time to choose her words carefully.

"What do you know about Alexandra?" she asked finally.

Blythe and Gage exchanged a look. He nodded, encouraging her to be the one to answer the question.

"I know that Walter Stern—the first Walter Stern—discovered her working at a casino in Havana and brought her to Hollywood to counter the popularity of MGM's Dietrich and Garbo. I also know that it worked. That critics and fans alike fell head over heels in love with her."

"Alexandra's exotic Russian looks were a striking contrast to the lacquered blondes of the day," Natasha said with a knowing nod.

"I know Stern cast her in femme fatale roles," Blythe continued, "which earned fines from the Hays commission and advisories of boycotts by the National Legion of Decency."

"Her waterfall scene in *Lady Reckless* was so hot, Louella Parsons said it was a miracle the celluloid film hadn't burned," Natasha told them with another faint, reminiscent smile. "Alexandra told me that Walter liked taking advantage of the fact that women fantasized about *being* Alexandra, while men fantasized about getting her into their beds."

Her still-bright gaze moved slowly over Blythe's face. "It is, of course, much the same marketing strategy that Walter's grandson has used with your pictures."

"Actually, I'm hoping to change that image," Blythe said. "Which is why I'm so interested in making this film."

"Yes." Natasha nodded again, thoughtful. "I can understand why you wish to make this film. The question is, will Stern permit it?"

"It isn't going to be his decision," Blythe revealed. "Since he's no longer in control of Xanadu Studios."

"You're joking!" Natasha leaned forward, her body a taut, tense line. "When did this happen?"

"Very recently." Blythe shook her head. "Connor Mackay, of C. S. Mackay Enterprises bought controlling interest in Xanadu. Connor told me, before I left for this trip, that he was about to send Walter packing."

"Amazing." Natasha leaned back in her chair and seemed to be considering that for a long time. "I wonder ... " Her voice drifted off. Her gaze turned inward.

"Wonder what?" Blythe asked when her nerves couldn't stand the waiting any longer. Her impatient question earned a sharp, warning look from Gage, reminding her what Cait had once said about successful interrogation being more about knowing when to keep quiet than when to ask questions.

Natasha looked at Blythe with a bit of surprise, as if she'd forgotten the couple existed. "I wonder if it's finally safe to tell."

She'd garnered even Gage's complete attention. "Are you saying you know who killed Alexandra?"

"I know who I've always suspected. But I have no proof."

"You don't believe Patrick killed her?" Gage asked.

Natasha snorted and muttered a curse in Russian. "Of course Patrick didn't murder Alexandra. He adored her." Her emerald eyes turned dreamy. "No woman was ever so loved by any man."

Excitement surged through Blythe. Natasha's declaration only seconded what she'd known all along. She leaned forward and put her hand on the elderly woman's lace clad knee. "Anything you can tell us," she said earnestly, "will be a big help."

Natasha gave her a sharp, direct look. "Are you seeking help with your screenplay? Or in clearing Patrick's name?"

"Both," Gage and Blythe said in unison. They exchanged a quick, surprised glance. Then a grin. Once again, their thoughts were on the same track.

"I knew," Natasha said, her voice sounding as if it were coming from a long distance away, like from the bottom of a wine dark sea, "the night of the party, that there would be trouble."

"The New Year's Eve party, at William Randolph Hearst's Palisades Beach Road house," Blythe couldn't keep herself from coaxing when Natasha fell silent again. "The night she was killed."

"Yes." The former makeup woman's distant gaze was filled with ancient pain. "I'd known Walter was orchestrating problems between Alexandra and Patrick, of course. Until that night, I'd hesitated putting myself at risk by interfering. But then I witnessed the unhappy results of all that wicked, behind the scenes manipulating."

"So Alexandra and Patrick did fight that night?"

"Yes. And it was a terrible scene. Alexandra looked, as always, stunning. She'd borrowed an evening gown from the studio wardrobe department, the same one she'd worn in Patrick's film, *Fool's Gold*. It was white satin, cut low and flowed over her perfectly sculpted ballerina's body like mercury, shimmering like the inside of a seashell in the streaming silver moonlight.

"The clinging satin dipped dangerously below her waist, leaving her back bare. It was, of course, obvious to everyone that she was wearing nothing beneath the dress."

"Patrick must have been jealous," Gage suggested.

"Perhaps." Natasha dipped her head. "But, I think he understood that other men would always want Alexandra. I also believe that such admiration didn't disturb him. So long as he was the man she always went home with."

Natasha frowned. "They did not go home together that night."

"They didn't?" Blythe felt a frisson of excitement mixed with fear. "What happened? Surely she wouldn't have left with another man?" She couldn't have, Blythe knew, with a certainty that went all the way to the bone. Not feeling the way she did about her husband.

"Of course not," Natasha said firmly, confirming Blythe's thoughts. "There was never another man for Alexandra. From the moment she first saw Patrick." Her gaze moved from Blythe to Gage, then back to Blythe. "Sometimes it works that way. As I believe you both know."

Blythe felt the damning color rising again in her cheeks. "I didn't realize it was that obvious."

Even Gage had to laugh. Anyone with eyes could see exactly how Blythe had spent the night. Her face was rosy and roughened from his beard, her swollen lips appeared almost bee stung, and the lingering glow in her dark eyes hinted at erotic pleasures.

"My dear," Natasha said with a gentle smile, "you must never apologize for being well loved." She flicked her braid over her shoulder. "It's a gift to be treasured."

One of the ways Blythe had survived a lifetime in Hollywood was keeping her private life exactly that. *Private.* Uncomfortable with discussing her relationship with Gage with this woman, who, although seemingly quite nice, was still a stranger, she returned the conversation to their reason for having come to Greece in the first place.

"Tell us about the argument," she prompted gently.

"Ah." Natasha sighed again. "Alexandra left the party first. Patrick was right behind her. He was tall, his stride so long, it took him no time at all to catch up with her. Her silver high heels were not made for walking in the sand and I remember him taking hold of her arm when she stumbled. But she shook off his touch and kept walking."

When Natasha closed her eyes, Blythe suspected she was seeing that long-ago night. "Patrick, unfortunately, had a furious temper. As did Alexandra."

"He grabbed her by the shoulders and spun her around. He was towering over her, his hands curved around her shoulders. He looked huge and threatening, even from a distance."

She opened her eyes and looked straight at Gage. "Now that I think about it, you remind me a great deal of Patrick Reardon."

"Gage doesn't have a temper," Blythe argued.

Natasha gave him a long look. "Of course he does, dear," she responded mildly. "You just haven't witnessed it, yet."

For what he suspected was a shot in the dark, she'd hit damn close to the bull's-eye. Since he didn't know how to respond to the calmly-stated accusation, Gage didn't say anything.

"Patrick was a mystery man, which, of course made him even more exciting," Natasha revealed. "When Walter brought him to Hollywood, to write the screenplay of his novel, the studio put out its typical glossy biography.

"According to Xanadu's publicity department, besides rounding up cattle, Patrick had also been a boxer in his youth, earning the money which allowed him to write by knocking people out in western bars. That was the official line. When he first arrived in town, rumors circulated that he'd killed a man with his bare hands."

"Rumors that proved to be false," Blythe pointed out. Gage had disproved that colorful story his first day on the job.

"True. But since Patrick refused to either confirm or deny the stories, they persisted."

"You were telling us about the night of the party," Gage prompted gently.

"I'd come out on the terrace for some fresh air. I watched them. Their faces were close together, but their taut angry poses were definitely not that of lovers. They exchanged words. Angry words I could not hear.

"Then Alexandra slapped Patrick across the cheek. For a moment, I feared he was actually going to strike her back. But he didn't.

"Instead, he dropped his hand to his side. Then, without another word, he went striding back toward the house. Alexandra called out to him. When he didn't respond, she threw the champagne glass at his back. Then she dropped to her knees in the soft sand and buried her face in her hands."

"That's the same thing she did in *Lady Reckless*," Blythe remembered. "When her married lover chose to return to his pregnant wife."

"I remember thinking that at the time," Natasha said. "But I knew that Alexandra was not acting. It was obvious that her weeping was all too real."

"Do you know what they were arguing about?" Blythe asked.

"I assumed some of it was about Alexandra's earlier life. When she was living in Cuba. You know, of course, that she was not really a Romanov."

"I'd assumed that the studio publicity department made her a member of the Russian family for box office appeal," Blythe said.

"That's exactly what they did. But, like many stories, it carried a nugget of truth. She *was* a Russian émigré. There were various versions of how she'd ended up in Cuba. Along with rumors that she'd done more than model bathing suits in those Havana casinos."

Since Gage had already uncovered the allegations during a recent trip to Florida, Blythe was not surprised by the statement. "Did Patrick know about these rumors?"

"I don't think so. Not in the beginning. But one day, shortly before the party, Walter Stern came to Alexandra's dressing room when I was making her up. He looked furious. He told me to leave, which I did. But I will admit to being worried about Alexandra, so I remained outside. Just in case she needed help. Stern was not," she said, her lips tightening, "a very nice man."

"So you heard what they discussed?"

"No. I thought I heard some mention of Havana, but the door was too thick to make out what they were saying. Then, shortly after I'd left them alone, the assistant director came to call Alexandra to the set. I was forced to redo her makeup. Because Stern had made her cry.

"It was obvious he was creating problems between Patrick and Alexandra. It was also obvious, from some of the things I'd witnessed, that he was trying to make Patrick believe that Alexandra was an unfaithful wife. At the same time Stern was using a contract actress to make Alexandra believe the same of Patrick." She

dragged her palms down a face that was remarkably un-
lined, given her age. "Unfortunately, the party was too
public a place to reveal such unsavory secrets. So I decided to tell her before the premiere of Patrick's film."

"A premiere she never attended," Gage said. "Because she was killed that night."

"Yes." Natasha's gaze was as dark and bleak as a tomb.
"And I've never forgiven myself for that. If only I'd gone
to her that night, if only I'd followed her home—"

"You can't second-guess yourself," Gage said. "It
doesn't do any good."

"I suppose not." Natasha sighed.

"There's something I don't understand," Blythe said.
"If you didn't believe Patrick killed Alexandra, if you
suspected you knew who did commit the crime, why
didn't you go to the police?"

"But I did," the elderly woman answered promptly. "I
also went to Patrick's attorney with my story. But I was
never called as a witness. Later, after Patrick was con-
victed, I realized that people far more powerful than me
wanted the story buried. Since I had no desire to end up
like Alexandra, I kept my silence. Later, despite my caution, I was fired for what I knew."

"I heard a different story."

"Of course you did." Natasha's smile was sad and
knowing at the same time. "You were told I was crazy. Or
a liar. Or both."

Blythe could not deny it. "Yes."

It was then Natasha Kuryan dropped her bombshell.
"I was fired by Walter Stern, Jr. because he was afraid
that someday I'd tell the truth. That his father, Alexandra's mentor, strangled her in an act of rage because she
was threatening to retire after the premiere of *Fool's Gold*

in order to move to Wyoming and live with her husband on his ranch."

That was definitely news. "Do you think she really would have done it?"

"Absolutely. In a heartbeat," Natasha confirmed. "It was obvious to everyone that Patrick hated Hollywood. It was also obvious that Alexandra loved Patrick. He was the sun around which her entire world revolved. If he wanted to return to Wyoming, she would not have hesitated leaving with him."

"But what about her career?" Gage asked. "Do you honestly believe she could turn her back on fame and success so easily?"

Accustomed to looking at all sides of a case, Gage felt obliged to consider the possibility that Alexandra, after having promised to leave Hollywood, found herself unable to go through with the planned move and ended up being killed by a furious husband—who possessed a deadly temper—for her change of mind.

Yet, even as he thought it, Gage also knew, with a deep-seated certainty that went all the way to the bone, that his conjecture had not been the case.

"Alexandra never cared for fame. Indeed, she often said it was the unfortunate price she was forced to pay for her beauty. She did possess an almost obsessive need for wealth," Natasha conceded. "But only because to her, money represented security. By the time Patrick met her, she had more money than she could have spent in several lifetimes. But, more importantly, he represented a security Alexandra had never known.

"I'm convinced, that had her life not been cut so tragically short, she would have left Hollywood with no regrets. And never looked back."

A heavy silence came over the room, settling over the trio like a wet, suffocating cloak. They were each immersed in their private thoughts of Alexandra when the door to the cabin burst open.

"Why is everyone so sad in the face?" Kyriako Papakosta asked in a big, booming voice. He entered the cabin on a long, strong stride, the energy of his personality sweeping away the gloom created by Natasha's tragic tale. "The sun is shining, it is a beautiful day." His teeth, beneath the shaggy white mustache flashed. "Much too nice to be down in the mouth.

"Besides," he complained to Natasha, "frowning will give you wrinkles." He brushed a huge beefy finger across her forehead.

"At my age, I'm no longer concerned about wrinkles," Natasha lied. "And Blythe is too young to worry."

"A few lines only give a stunning woman's face character." Kyriako quickly changed gears as he turned to Blythe with another flash of strong teeth.

"Of course I am familiar with your work," he said after Natasha introduced them. He took Blythe's outstretched hand and lifted it to his smiling lips. "And I've always found you as talented as you are lovely. But—" his smiling eyes turned suddenly serious "—I do not think your talent has been properly presented."

Romantic chivalry combined with honesty made an unusual and devastating combination. Blythe immediately understood why Natasha Kuryan had jumped ship to remain behind in Greece.

"I'm working on that," she said with an answering smile.

"Ah, yes." His hearty face, tanned to a deep hazelnut by eight decades of Mediterranean sun, took on a momentarily grave expression. "Natasha told me about your

Alexandra Romanov problem. It's a very sad story. I remember being quite distraught when she died. She was so lovely. And so young."

He turned and shook Gage's hand. "And you are the man who intends to solve the murder. After all these years."

"So you don't think Patrick killed Alexandra, either?" Blythe asked.

The older man snorted. "Of course not. I know of no one who believed that cock-and-bull story the prosecution presented. It was obvious that Alexandra's novelist husband was, how do you Americans put it, railroaded?"

"That's the word, all right," Gage agreed with a frown that revealed he wasn't fond of thinking that the system of justice he'd spent the major part of his adult life defending could be so badly misused. "And unfortunately, I'm beginning to agree with you."

"Of course you are," Kyriako said. "Everyone always agrees with Papakosta, because he is always right. Isn't that correct, my golden one?" he asked Natasha.

"Of course," she answered on cue, drawing a laugh all around.

"You must let me give you the grand tour," Kyriako proclaimed. "Then we will have breakfast."

Not a single person in the room felt inclined to argue.

8

AFTER A TOUR of the luxurious yacht, followed by breakfast and lively conversation with the ebullient Greek author, Blythe and Gage returned to the hotel where they spent a long, indulgent time making slow, dreamy love.

Later that afternoon, desire temporarily sated, they were sitting side by side on the balcony outside her bedroom, looking out over the cerulean sea. Gage had his arm around Blythe's shoulders; her head was resting on his.

"Do you think it's possible?" Blythe asked. Hours after meeting the elderly Russian makeup artist, her mind was still spinning with the possibilities. "Do you believe Walter Stern really could have been the murderer?"

"Someone kept Natasha from testifying," Gage said carefully. As a cop, he'd always believed that jumping to conclusions led to dangerous—and often embarrassing—landings. "Someone with power and connections."

"Someone like the head of a major motion picture studio." Blythe shook her head. "I can't believe he'd take such a risk. It doesn't make any sense."

Gage ran his hand down her hair. Pressed his lips against her temple. "Crimes of passion seldom do." Because it had been too long since he'd kissed her—at least ten minutes—he cupped her chin between his thumb and

finger and lifted her lips to his. "Speaking of passion . . ."

It was happening again. Despite the fact that they'd
spent most of the afternoon in her bed, Blythe found
herself wanting Gage all over again. When he slipped his
tongue between her parted lips to seduce hers, Blythe felt
herself melting, like a wax candle left out too long in the
unrelenting Mediterranean sun.

"Oh, yes," she said on a long, blissful sigh as he carried her through the French doors, into the adjoining
bedroom. It was the last thing she would say for a very
long time.

*IT WAS NEARLY midnight. A white moon rose in a star-
spangled sky, creating a silvery path on the darkened
waters of the ocean below. The unceasing sound of the
incoming tide lapped softly against the glistening sand;
the sea breeze rustled in the tops of the palm trees. Smoke
from the smudge pots that nearby orange growers
burned during these winter nights to warm their groves,
wafted on the salt air. With the exception of that faint
odor of smoke—and the sight of a woman, stumbling
across the beach—it could have been another perfect
night in Lotus Land.*

*"Dammit!" Alexandra cursed as her silver high heels
bogged down in the thick dry sand, causing her to twist
her ankle. She would have fallen, had it not been for the
strong hand reaching from the darkness to grab her arm.*

*"Let go of me," she shouted, shaking free of the pos-
sessive masculine touch. "I don't want you to touch me.
Ever again."*

*"You don't mean that." His voice was deep and rich
and, dammit, as exciting as ever.*

"Yes, I do!"

She was wearing her thick sable hair loose and flowing, her trademark mermaid waves attractively ruffled by the sea breeze. When some of those strands blew across her face, he brushed them away with fingers far gentler than she would have expected, given the circumstance.

"You're a horrid man." Her accent thickened when she was emotional and tonight Alexandra was more upset than she could ever remember being. His fingers were still on her cheek; when she batted them away, her wedding ring glittered in the moonlight. "You're a liar. And a cheat."

She lifted the champagne glass she was carrying and with a dramatic flair, downed the remainder of the sparkling wine. "I wish I'd never met you."

Patrick looked inclined to touch her again, but instead slipped his hands into the pockets of his dress slacks. "You're talking to the man you love," he reminded her.

"That's not even an original line," she shot back. "Clark Gable said it to Norma Shearer in A Free Soul."

Patrick shrugged, drawing her unwilling attention to the way his broad shoulders strained the seams of his custom-tailored white dinner jacket. "A good writer knows enough to steal a great line when he hears one."

Her temper reaching the boiling point, Alexandra categorically refused to let her husband defuse her anger. Not after having caught him in that clinch with Mae Chandler, the actress Walter was touting for an Oscar for her supporting role as the long-suffering wife in Alexandra's latest film, Lady Reckless. Typecast as usual, Alexandra had, of course, played the man's backstreet mistress.

"Not that you'd know anything about good writing," she spat out, her words meant to wound.

Anger flashed in his eyes. "It's not how it looked," he said mildly.

She tossed her head. "That must be one of your own lines. Since it's trite and overused."

A muscle clenched in his jaw, revealing that she'd just gone too far. "Speaking of being overused," he said in a low voice that she recognized as being more dangerous than a shout, "since you seem to be all worked up about my alleged infidelity, how would you like to discuss your own recent dalliances?"

She drew in a deep, painful breath. That was a lie. There'd never been anyone else for her since she'd first laid eyes on Patrick Reardon.

Refusing to dignify the accusation—which he had obviously only thrown out to muddy the waters after being caught kissing some opportunistic slut—Alexandra said, "I have nothing to discuss with you."

Patrick was towering over his wife, looking huge and threatening. He lowered his head until his face was close to hers.

"That's too damn bad. Because I have a great deal to talk about with you. Beginning with your stint as one of Havana's premiere whores."

He could have hurt her no less if he'd reached out one of those strong dark fists and hit her in the solar plexus. Alexandra's creamy complexion turned as white as the moonlight streaming down around them.

"I don't know what you're talking about," she hedged, frantically wondering who'd told him about her less than pristine life in Cuba.

Certainly not Walter? Alexandra knew that the studio head was furious about her marriage, claiming it di-

minished her sex appeal, which in turn, hurt box office
receipts. But a year after eloping with Patrick, there was
still not another star who equaled her drawing power—
not Garbo or Dietrich, or even that lacquered blond
bombshell, Jean Harlow.

Vindictive as Walter admittedly could be, possessive
as he'd always been, Alexandra couldn't believe he'd risk
the story getting out that Xanadu's most popular star was
a former prostitute.

"For an actress, you're a rotten liar, sweetheart," Patrick shot back. "But, now that I think about it, I suppose it's not all that different, selling your body for pesos
above some Havana casino, or trading it for starring
roles in Tinseltown."

On a roll, he ignored her furious gasp. "The problem
is, it makes a guy kind of wonder—" his gaze was iced
fury as it raked its way over her still flat stomach "—exactly whose bun you've got in your oven."

Alexandra had not had an easy life. Until coming to
America, her entire existence had been a seemingly con-
tinuous pattern of deprivation, pain and loss. She'd been
five years old when World War I broke out, eight when
a revolution ended czarist rule and led to civil war. She'd
lost her father during a peasant uprising, one brother was
killed in the Red Army, another was imprisoned and later
died after a sailors' revolt at the naval base near Petro-
grad.

She and her mother had been driven off their land, but
not before her mother had first been brutally raped by
the soldiers sent to claim the farm for the Bolsheviks.
Held back by arms far stronger than hers, Alexandra had
been forced to watch. Two weeks later her mother died,
more, Alexandra believed, from a broken heart than
from the pain the soldiers had inflicted on her body.

She spent the next five years laboring eighteen hours a day on collective farms. The work was hard, she received no pay and the scant bit of food she was allowed barely kept her from starving. Prone to daydreaming, she was also beaten with depressing regularity.

When her ugly duckling stick-thin frame blossomed into a swan's voluptuous curves, Alexandra realized that her body, and her face, were her fortune. And her means of survival.

By her sixteenth birthday, she'd become mistress to a high-ranking politburo member. Two years later, she bribed the captain of a merchant vessel with sex—and money stolen from her lover—to take her out of the country. He'd willingly agreed, then kept her captive the entire voyage to Cuba, doing excruciating, hateful things to her body and her spirit.

Oh, Alexandra had known pain, all right. But never could she have imagined that mere words could hurt more than the pain so many men in her past had already inflicted on her. She'd come to view the baby she and Patrick had made together as a miracle—a reward for surviving all the past sins committed against her. For Patrick to even dare question that it was his child was unthinkable!

"You bastard!" She slapped him. Hard. The sound reverberated like a gunshot in the perfumed night air.

Patrick raised his own dark hand and for a long, suspended moment, although he'd only ever touched her in passion, or with heartbreaking tenderness, Alexandra actually believed he would strike her back.

Their eyes met. And held. Then Patrick muttered a low, vicious curse and slowly lowered his hand to his side. Without another word, he turned abruptly on his heel and went marching back toward the house.

"Patrick!" They couldn't leave it like this. "Please! Come back!"

Her words were whipped away by the wind. Confused and hurt and upset, she hurled the champagne glass at his rigid, departing back.

Then she dropped to her knees and buried her face in her hands.

Blythe woke with a start, the sob of some long distant pain caught in her throat. Lying beside her, Gage was instantly jerked from a sound sleep.

"BLYTHE?" He reached out and touched her wet face. "It's okay, sweetheart," he soothed. "It was only a bad dream."

"Oh, Gage!" She flung herself into his arms and pressed her cheek against the reassuring strength of his chest. "It seemed so real."

The tears were streaming down her face. He could feel them, hot and wet against his naked flesh. He smoothed his palm down her sleep-tousled hair. "You were dreaming about Alexandra." It was not a question.

She burrowed deeper, like a kitten trying to escape a thunderstorm. "It was as if I were there. The night of the party. The night she was murdered."

She was trembling. His hands continued their caresses down her back, his touch meant to soothe, rather than arouse. "That's not surprising," he murmured against the top of her head. "Considering what Natasha told us today. Yesterday," he amended as he viewed the stuttering pale light of a rosy new dawn slipping between the shutters.

"You don't understand." Tilting her head back, she looked up at him, her eyes glistening with moisture. "I know what they were arguing about."

"Natasha said they were probably arguing about Alexandra's time in Havana," he reminded her gently. He brushed her hair away from her face and kissed her temple. The slanted line of her cheekbone. Her lips.

His touch, his mouth, his reassuring tone, all conspired to calm her. But they could not make Blythe question the validity of what she knew. "She was right. Patrick did accuse her of being a whore." She wrapped her arms around him and felt safe. "But then it got even worse.... Alexandra was pregnant."

"There was no mention of that in either the autopsy report or the trial."

"I don't care what the official report says. I know it's true." Blythe began shivering again as she recalled, in vivid detail, Patrick's frigid, unrelenting glare. "Patrick told her that he didn't believe the child she was carrying was his."

The words rang a deep and distant chord. An icy fist clenched at his heart. Concerned with the way Blythe was trembling, like a frail leaf in a hurricane, Gage didn't allow himself to dwell on it.

"It was a nightmare," he repeated soothingly. "Only a bad dream."

"No." Blythe shook her head. "You don't understand—"

He didn't want to hear it. "I understand you've been under a great deal of stress. I understand that you haven't been getting enough sleep. Which," he said as his lips brushed against hers again, lingering for a moment, "is mostly my fault, at least these past two nights."

As Blythe clung even tighter to him, her breasts flattened against his chest, her lips burrowed into the hollow of his throat, Gage began finding it difficult to keep his mind on this conversation. She felt so good. So warm. So right.

"It's not at all surprising that your subconscious would start filling in the blanks, sweetheart."

"That's exactly what's happening." She lifted her eyes to his again, her gaze grave. "But it's real, Gage. As if it's happening to me. Not Alexandra."

"You were dreaming," he insisted.

The mists had cleared from her mind, leaving her with a clarity as bright as a new day. "Then tell me one thing."

"If I can."

"Did any of the information you uncovered reveal how Alexandra got to Cuba in the first place?"

"No, but—"

"She bribed a captain of a merchant ship to take her out of Russia. It was not an easy voyage. He abused her. Unmercifully."

Blythe's gaze took on a distant, faraway look. "When the ship landed in Cuba to pick up sugar cane, I left the captain's quarters for the first time since we'd set sail from Odessa."

Gage immediately caught the change in her words. "Blythe—"

"For the first time in my life," she said, ignoring his murmured interruption, "I was truly free." She looked up at him. "You Americans have no idea what that word means. You take it for granted."

Impossible as it was, she'd begun speaking with a Russian accent. Even as he didn't understand why he was witnessing this performance, Gage reminded himself that Blythe was a superb actress.

"For the first time in my life, I was free from the grinding poverty and degradation that had been my life in Russia," Blythe continued.

"It felt marvelous." Her full dark lips curved that sexy, trademark smile capable of bringing any red-blooded male to his knees. "Although the city was overrun with beautiful women, I immediately got a job modeling swim suits in the casinos for rich old men who stank of rum and cigar smoke. If, on occasion, I did more than model, if some small-minded persons might accuse me of being a *prastitootka*, I refuse to apologize."

She lifted her head with a haughty pride suggesting the former Czarina the studio publicity machine had made Alexandra out to be. Her eyes flashed jet sparks. "Survival is something only the rich take lightly."

Gage stared down at her, transfixed. Before his eyes, she'd literally become Alexandra Romanov. It was more than a mere physical resemblance. More than a mimicking of her voice and body language. What he was witnessing was Alexandra's spirit. Her soul.

"When Walter Stern came to me in Havana, and asked me if I had ever acted on the stage, I had to laugh. I was, of course, already, in my own fashion, a premiere *aktrisa*."

She tossed her dark head; defiance blazed in her ebony eyes. "Of course, my stage was not in a theater, but in a luxuriously appointed suite in the city's finest tourist hotel. And my rapt and appreciative audience was only one man at a time."

Her gaze fixed on Gage. "You dare to accuse me of betraying you, but you do not attempt to appreciate what it was like for me, for so many of us, after the revolution. We have a saying in my country—'A sated man cannot understand a starving one.'" Her furious eyes raked over him.

"You have said you love me. But I believe you only fell in love with the glamorous woman on that large silver screen. Not the very human woman who carries your child."

A chill crept into Gage, going deep into the bone. "Blythe." He took hold of her shoulders and shook her. Lightly, at first. Then, when he received no response, harder. His fingers tightened. Gage knew there'd be bruises, but at this moment, he honestly didn't care. "Dammit, Blythe, it's me, sweetheart. Gage."

It was his tone, more than his words, that filtered through the fog clouding her mind. He sounded frightened. More than frightened, she realized with amazement. Terrified.

The painful memory faded from her eyes before she closed them on a soft, ragged moan.

She struggled against the almost overwhelming desire to remain where she was. But her need for Gage, her love for him, pulled her back.

"Gage?" She blinked against the blinding light of the sun that was rising from the sea outside the window. Her eyes felt dry and scratchy, their lids leaden. Her tongue was thick.

"Got it on the first try." Not even attempting to hide his relief, he lowered his forehead to hers. "Lord, lady, you had me terrified half out of my wits for a while there."

His relief flowed out of him and into her, metamorphosing to a soothing warmth that made Blythe realize exactly how lucky she was to have this man in her life.

Vowing that she'd never let anything—or anyone—come between them, she lifted her lips to his. Their mouths met in a desperate, mutual pleasure as Blythe allowed the glory of his kiss to dull the last lingering vestiges of pain.

The fever rose, as it always did. As she knew it always would. Wanting to show him how much she loved him, how much she'd always love him, Blythe wrapped her arms around him and pushed him back down to the mattress.

Strong, willful, her hands skimmed over his naked body, drawing husky, hungry groans as they never lingered on any one spot for very long. The room was cast in a golden morning glow. The air swirling hotly around them was rich and redolent with the perfume of the jasmine outside the window, the scent of desire emanating from love-warmed flesh.

The power built inside her. Blythe's need for Gage was as urgent as breath. And every bit as vital. As they rolled over the bed, tangling the sheets, her mouth streaked over him, following the heated path her hands had blazed, greedily tasting, savoring, loving.

Hot hammers of need pounded inside him. The control he'd always counted on had deserted him, stripped away by the fever of her mouth, the tempest of her hands. For the first time in his thirty-one years Gage felt utterly helpless.

Half-mad, his breath burning in his lungs, his loins, he grasped hold of her waist with unsteady hands as she straddled his hips. "Now," he said, lifting her above him.

Her eyes were dark with passion, but a flame burned in their midnight depths. "Now." Their eyes met, exchanging unspoken promises as she lowered herself onto him, taking him inside her, steel into warm satin.

Her body contracted as he filled her, her muscles clenching, throbbing. He watched the naked thrill rise in her eyes.

"I love you, Blythe." The words came hoarsely from his throat.

"And I love you." He was hers. Body, mind, heart. The unquestioning knowledge sent a new warmth surging through her—an emotional joy that increased the physical pleasure. "Only you." Her lips were full and parted. Her damp flesh glistened in the gilt morning light. She gripped his wrists, lifting his willing hands to her breasts. "Always."

Her hair curtained both their faces as she lowered her mouth to his. The sun was warm on her back as they rose together, the ancient rhythm instinctive, perfect.

MUCH, MUCH LATER, they were back in the horse-drawn carriage, on the way to the waterfront. Although neither was anxious to leave the romantic island, both reluctantly agreed that the clock was ticking. Even if Connor would be willing to change the shooting schedule on *Expose*, which was a possibility, it was still imperative Blythe return to work on the project.

As for Gage, Blythe knew she was not his only client. And even with Lily having recently become his partner, she understood his need to return to the states.

Even knowing all that, as she watched their cliff-side hotel growing smaller and smaller in the distance, Blythe found herself wishing that one of them wasn't so damn responsible.

"I've made a decision," Gage said abruptly.

His gruff tone unnerved her, just a little. "Oh?"

"I'm still willing to let you get used to the idea of marriage. But I want us to live together."

She immediately relaxed. "I'm already packed."

"Are you saying you're willing to move in with me? Just like that?" As comfortable as Bachelor Arms was, it was still a long way from Blythe's Beverly Hills mansion.

"For the time being," she agreed. "At least until my house is restored. Then perhaps, if you're comfortable with the idea, we can move in there and keep your apartment as your office."

"Whatever you want." Having expected her to put up an argument, Gage was pleased and admittedly relieved at her immediate acquiescence. He didn't care where the hell they lived so long as they were together. Hopefully, once they were living under the same roof, she'd realize that marriage was the only logical next step.

"Until then, as nice as the Chateau Marmont is, since I'm a little tired of living in a hotel, I love the idea of moving into Bachelor Arms with you."

He threaded his hands through her hair and grinned down into her face. That breathtakingly lovely face that had been haunting his sleep for months. "Are you saying you just want me for my apartment?"

Laughing merrily, she lifted her smiling lips to his. "Believe me, darling," she murmured against his mouth, "of all the reasons I want you, your apartment, as charming as it admittedly is, is very far down on my list."

They'd reached the dock. At the driver jumped down from the front seat and began unloading their luggage from the back of the carriage, Blythe reluctantly broke off the kiss.

"You've made a list?" Gage asked, knowing Blythe's penchant for details. He climbed out of the carriage.

"Of course," she said as he lifted her down to the ground,

They were standing there, beside the clear blue water, bathed in the warmth of the morning sun, his hands on her waist, hers on his shoulders. Blythe found herself wishing she could stop time, like a movie freeze-frame.

"Don't you think I should see this alleged list? So I can have an idea what's expected of me?"

"As soon as we get home, we can begin working our way through it," she promised. Laughter and what he knew to be love danced in her eyes. "One night at a time."

"Hey, you're the boss," he agreed.

9

"THIS IS GOOD STUFF," Sloan Wyndham told Blythe the morning after her return from Los Angeles. Although she'd had less than five hours' sleep, she'd been eager to share the information she'd gleaned during her trip to Greece.

They were sitting in his office, which took up several hundred square feet of his Pacific Palisades home. The wall of floor-to-ceiling windows overlooked the sparkling expanse of ocean. Each time she visited, Blythe wondered how anyone could get any work done when faced with such a dazzling view. The fact that Sloan had actually progressed so well on the Alexandra screenplay said as much about his power of concentration as it did his talent.

Since a rewarding string of successes had put the maverick screenwriter in the upper echelons of hot properties in Hollywood—making him one of a few "bankable" writer-directors in the business—scarcely a day went by that Blythe didn't consider herself fortunate that he'd agreed to sign on to her project.

"Personally, I thought it was horribly sad," she contradicted him quietly.

The grin faded from his handsome face. "True. But it definitely fills in a lot of missing blanks." He leaned back in his leather chair, linked his hands together behind his head and eyed her with admiration. "Obviously, Natasha proved as helpful as you and Gage had hoped."

"Yes." Blythe didn't tell him that her knowledge of the facts of the argument had not come entirely from the elderly makeup woman, but from some deep-seated source she could not explain.

"The thing we have to decide now is whether we should fictionalize the story so we can suggest a killer, or keep it factual, go with what we've got, and leave the mystery unsolved."

As it had remained for so many years. Too many years.

Blythe knew what she wanted to do. She also knew that coming out and implying Walter Stern may have murdered his studio's biggest star could get her into legal hot water. Especially since having just lost the studio that had been in his family for three generations, Walter Stern III wouldn't take kindly to another attack on his family. He was not a man to cross lightly.

"Let me discuss it with legal," she suggested.

"Terrific." Sloan's scowl, as he dragged a hand through his shaggy chestnut hair, reminded Blythe of something he'd said when she'd first asked him to work on the project with her.

"I recall you comparing the director's role to that of a sculptor, chiseling away at the stone, ultimately setting the vision—and the truth—free," she murmured. "You also said that you categorically refused to expend creative energy on a story only to let some guy with a chain saw loose on it."

His scowl turned to a grin. "I was pretty much of a self-important, egotistical bastard that day, wasn't I?"

Blythe shrugged. "I understood that you wanted to maintain control. To ensure that when the picture was finished, whatever was born from that beginning block of marble would be *your* vision."

"And yours," he pointed out.

"Yes." She knew what he was getting at, understood he was warning her not to let fear of litigation dilute the strength of the story she'd wanted to tell for so long.

During these recent months working closely together, Blythe had discovered that the stories of Sloan Wyndham's impatience and fierce independence, which routinely landed him in hot water with studio executives, were not exaggerated. She knew he found her caution unreasonably frustrating.

"Gage is trying to track down the detectives who'd been the first to arrive at the murder scene that morning," she revealed. "Why don't we give him a few more days?"

"And if he doesn't find them?"

Blythe hated feeling so uncharacteristically hesitant. "He'll find them."

He studied her, looking long, looking deep. "I remember thinking, the first time we met, that this project was very personal to you."

She thought of the dreams. The nightmares. "That's become an understatement."

"So Cait has said." Concern rose in his whiskey brown eyes as he studied the smudged purple shadows beneath her eyes. "I also asked you, that first day, if you were hiring me to write a screenplay, solve a murder, or right a sixty-year-old wrong. Do you remember what you answered?"

How could she forget? It was a question she asked herself for weeks. For months.

"At the time, I told you," Blythe said slowly, "that I thought all three."

"And now?"

She dragged her hand through her hair, feeling unreasonably nervous. "Although I don't have a thread of hard evidence, or any concrete proof, I know, without a shadow of a doubt, that Patrick didn't kill Alexandra." Unwilling to meet his probing gaze, she looked out over the gleaming, sun-brightened water. "You probably think I'm crazy."

"Hell, yes."

"What?" Her head spun back toward him.

"Anyone working in this business is crazy," he explained with a quick, easy grin that Blythe suspected was part of the reason Cait had fallen for him. "You, me, hell, this entire town is nuts. If movies didn't exist, we'd all probably have to be locked away in padded rooms."

Blythe laughed, as she was supposed to. The tense mood passed. She rose from her chair with a lithe grace, bent over and kissed him on the cheek. "Cait's a lucky woman."

Another grin reached his dancing brown eyes. "I remind her of that every day. Right after I consider the irony of having fallen head over heels in love with a woman who'd held me at gunpoint the first time we met."

Having been present for that little episode, Blythe grinned as well. "Ah, the perils of falling for a cop."

"It's not that bad," Sloan assured her as he walked her to the front door. "While I'm still not wild about the Glock, I've discovered that handcuffs present a realm of intriguing possibilities." His touch on her back was light and friendly. "You should ask Gage if he still has an old pair hanging around from his days on the force."

Blythe laughed, as he'd intended.

But as she drove down the steep and winding road back toward Sunset, Blythe found herself almost considering adding Sloan's outrageous—albeit admittedly erotic—suggestion to her list.

"You just missed him," Lily greeted Blythe when she arrived at Gage's Bachelor Arms apartment. "He's on his way to the airport."

"The airport? But we've only been back from Greece a few hours."

"I know. But we had a lead on one of the men he was looking for."

"You've found one of the detectives?" Blythe had been frustrated to learn that the two men had quit the force and left town two weeks after the murder. Unperturbed, Gage had assured her that Lily's natural born talent for spelunking in the dark caverns of public records was nothing short of remarkable.

"It looks like it. Unless it's a different Michael Connelly. Which it could be," Lily warned. "It's not that uncommon a name, after all. But the man *is* a former county deputy. The fact that he was in law enforcement is a link."

"I wish Gage had waited for me," Blythe complained. "I'd hoped to be along when he questioned him."

"He wasn't trying to keep you out of things," Lily assured her quickly. "It's just that Connelly's scheduled to leave on a fishing trip out of state first thing tomorrow morning. Gage wanted to wait for you, but he only had thirty minutes to catch his flight."

"What is it with elderly people these days?" Blythe muttered. "Don't any of them stay home in their rocking chairs where they belong?"

"Hey, don't knock it," Lily said with a laugh. "Every time I get behind one of those motor homes on the freeway, it gives me hope that I'll still be having fun in my old age."

"If this investigation goes on much longer, I'm going to be old before my time." Drawn to the oversize pewter-framed mirror, Blythe scowled at her reflection. "Look at this," she complained. "I've actually got a gray hair."

"Where?" Lily came and stood beside her, looking into the mirror as well. "I don't see anything."

"Right here." Blythe plucked a hair from her temple. "See?"

"Lord," Lily said, "you're right. Well, you'd better not let Gage find out. He'll dump you for sure."

Blythe laughed. "All right, maybe I am exaggerating. But the longer I'm on this project, the more frustrating it gets." She gave up looking for additional gray hairs and returned their conversation back to its original track. "So where, exactly is Gage off to?"

"Oregon. Connelly's got a retirement cabin at Lake of the Woods, outside of Klamath Falls."

"How on earth did you find him there?"

"It wasn't that hard. I simply ran a check of former law enforcement pension recipients in neighboring states and found a Connelly who'd retired after thirty years working for the Klamath County sheriff's department."

Believing that they were finally on the brink of solving the crime, Blythe hugged her long time friend. "Gage is right. You are a genius."

"Which is only one of the reasons I fell in love with her," a familiar voice said from the front door. Engrossed in conversation, neither Lily nor Blythe had heard Connor enter. The baby he was holding was dressed in a ruffly pink dress and white socks. An elastic band with a polka-dot pink bow adorned a head covered with blond fuzz that looked as soft as duck down.

"I hadn't realized it had gotten so late," Lily said, hurrying across the room to greet her fiancé. Their lips met over the baby's head. As the kiss lingered, Blythe felt a twinge of envy. As much as she wanted to solve the mystery of Alexandra's death, she'd also been looking forward to spending another night in Gage's arms.

"How did Katie like her first day at the studio?" Lily asked when the kiss ended,

"She was a hit with one and all," Connor said proudly. "In fact, she drew so much attention, I was tempted to sign her to a performing contract." He grinned down at the baby, who was sucking on a pink fist. Gazing up at him with crossed blue eyes, she flashed a toothless smile in return.

"But she informed me she'd much rather be behind a desk instead of in front of the camera."

Lily folded her arms across her chest. "She actually told you that?"

"Of course."

"I didn't realize infants could talk," Blythe said, enjoying the sight of the obviously happy family group.

"Most can't," Connor agreed easily. "But Katie is her mother's child. A genius. Aren't you, sweetheart?" He ran his hand over the top of the pale fuzz and was rewarded with happy baby gurgling. "See? She's telling you that she made me promise to begin grooming her to take over from her old man some day."

"Well, I'll certainly go along with that," Blythe said. "This town could use a lot more women heading up studios."

"Katie is going to grow up to be whatever she wants," Lily said firmly.

"Of course she will," Connor answered without missing a beat. "She can be a doctor, lawyer or a candlestick maker—"

"Don't forget mother."

"A mother?" Connor frowned as he gazed down into the round pink face, as if seeking the baby's future in her wide blue eyes. "That would mean letting some guy get his grubby hands on her."

"That's how it usually works," Blythe agreed, enjoying the way Connor had so effortlessly stepped into the role of father to Lily's child. From the moment he'd helped bring Katie into the world, it had been obvious that Connor could not have loved this baby more if she was his natural daughter.

"I don't suppose," he asked Lily, "that you'd be open to locking our Katie in a closet right now, then letting her out when she's thirty?"

"Not on a bet." The love and laughter in Lily's eyes belied her stern tone.

"I was afraid of that." Connor ran his knuckles down the infant's satiny cheek and sighed. "I suppose there's only one thing to do."

"I'm afraid to ask," Lily said, exchanging a look with Blythe.

The thirty-one-year-old millionaire that the *Wall Street Journal* had recently called a financial wunderkind with a Midas touch was brilliant, sexy, and as Lily had learned, incredibly generous and loving.

Growing up on a Kansas farm, with parents who'd instilled deep-seated, solid middle-class values into her, Lily also found Connor unnervingly impulsive. Not that the trait so different from her own serious approach to life had kept her from falling in love with him.

On the contrary, Lily thought now, although it was his kindness that had overcome the pain of her disastrous marriage, it had been Connor's dizzying freedom of spirit that had taught her exactly how high, and how far, she could fly.

"We'll just have to provide Katie with some brothers," Connor said. "The sooner the better."

"I don't understand—"

"It's really quite simple." Connor grinned, looking more than a little pleased with himself for having solved yet another of life's dilemmas. "I'll teach the boys to beat up any male that dares even look at Katie with lust in his beady little eyes."

Blythe laughed, remembering all the times when Lily had been steadfastly refusing his advances, that Connor's overtly hungry gaze had practically devoured the pregnant young woman.

"Don't knock lust, darling." Lily went up on her toes and brushed her lips against his again. "Especially if you want Katie to have all those brothers."

As their lips clung, Blythe felt another fleeting surge of envy and wished she was on that plane to Oregon with Gage.

How much her life had changed in the past three months, she mused. How much all their lives had changed!

As if reading her mind, Lily announced, "Blythe is moving in with Gage."

Connor grinned his approval. "It's about time."

Blythe rolled her eyes. "Why is it everyone refuses to acknowledge that I was engaged until just a few days ago?"

"Because no one believed you and the doc had one of those ever-after type of things going for you," Connor answered.

"Like you and Gage do," Lily tacked on. "All anyone had to do was see the two of you together to know that you were destined to be together."

Blythe thought back to something Kyriako Papakosta had said during their lunch. About the Greeks believing that character was destiny. "I don't know about destiny," she said. "But I do know I'm awfully glad he's in my life."

"Gage Remington is your fate," Lily insisted. "The same way Connor is mine." The couple exchanged a warm, intimate glance.

"Now, all we have to do is make it legal," Connor pointed out. "Which you keep putting off, I might add."

"I want to lose weight so I can fit into a wedding dress," Lily complained. "I want everything to be perfect."

"*You're* already perfect. *Katie's* perfect. I'm not, but fortunately, the two of you make up for it. Besides, we're also all perfect together, aren't we, Blythe?"

"Absolutely."

"So." He put his arm around her and drew her closer, embracing mother and daughter. "When the hell are you going to let me make an honest woman of you?"

"You're so busy right now," Lily demurred. "With the takeover at the studio, and—"

"When, Lily?" His friendly tone was laced with that same determination that had allowed him to overcome Lily's initial refusal, after her disastrous marriage, to have anything to do with any man. Especially a wealthy one.

Her answering laughter revealed that she knew she was about to give in. Again. "We'll talk about it tonight," she promised. "After I get home."

"I thought you'd come home with us."

"Actually, Cait and I are taking Blythe out to dinner."

"You are?" It was the first Blythe had heard of such plans.

"We both want to hear all about your trip," Lily said.

"What you're really interested in is what happened to make me break my engagement with Alan. And move in with Gage."

"That, too," Lily agreed cheerfully. "It's only fair, Blythe. Cait told me how you wouldn't rest until she ended up with Sloan and you certainly did your best to get Connor and me together. Now it's our turn to gang up on you."

Unable to argue with that reasoning, Blythe threw up her hands and caved in.

Lily and Cait had arranged to meet at Flynn's, the convivial bar next to Bachelor Arms. Flynn's served as a community watering hole—a place to sit and talk and share what had happened that day with neighbors.

"I saved your favorite booth," Bobbie-Sue O'Hara greeted Lily with a smile and a hug.

Although Lily hadn't known the waitress and part-time actress very well when they'd both been living at Bachelor Arms—before Lily had moved into the luxurious Malibu beach house Connor had bought for his new family—lately, as she'd continued to spend her days at the apartment building working with Gage, the two women had grown closer.

Often, when tracking down a deadbeat dad or runaway teenager, Lily needed to run downtown to some government agency who refused to hand over documentation without proper paperwork. On more than one such occasion, Bobbie-Sue had volunteered to babysit Katie.

And although a more cynical person might suggest that the actress was currying favor by helping out the fiancée of the new owner of Xanadu Studios, Lily knew that Bobbie-Sue was merely being a good neighbor.

"How was your trip?" Bobbie-Sue as Blythe as the women sat across from each other in the booth against the wall.

"It was lovely." Having heard that Bobbie-Sue liked to know everything that went on in the building, and not wanting to add grist to the gossip mill, Blythe did not go into either the blossoming of her relationship with Gage, or what she'd learned about Alexandra. "The weather was lovely, the sun shone the entire time and I ate too much."

"I visited Greece with my parents, during a tour of Europe when I was in high school," Bobbie-Sue said. "I have to admit, I got an enormous crush on this drop-dead gorgeous waiter."

Blythe laughed. "That seems to be a common teenage reaction to the country."

"I had a crush when I was in high school," Lily revealed. "On a painter. In Florence."

"A painter," Bobbie-Sue's blue eyes turned a little dreamy at the idea. "I think an Italian painter beats a Greek waiter."

"Actually, this was in Florence, Kansas." Lily's quick grin showed no trace of envy that unlike Bobbie-Sue or Blythe, the farthest she'd ever gotten from home before college was a weekend at the fair in Kansas City. Although she'd never lacked for the essentials, her parents had neither the time nor the funds for lengthy vacations.

Lily had been poor and she'd been rich. Then, as if life was some giant roller coaster, she'd lost all her money and soon, once she married Connor, she figured she'd be richer than ever. But, having been miserable as the wife of a lying, cheating scion to an old New York money family, and having fallen in love with Connor when she'd believed him to be just another struggling tenant of Bachelor Arms, Lily knew that love and loyalty were more important than wealth.

"Matt Stewart was a student at Kansas State Teachers College in Emporia," she continued. "The summer between his junior and senior years, he painted my Daddy's barn." She braced her elbows on the table, rested her chin in her linked fingers and grinned wickedly. "I've probably exaggerated in my mind over the years how handsome he was, but I'd just finished reading a book on art history, and I remember thinking that Matt's bare chest made Michelangelo's David look downright puny."

Blythe and Bobbie-Sue both laughed.

"Now I wish my parents had taken us to Kansas," Bobbie-Sue complained on the soft drawl that often led people to mistakenly believe she was just another cheerleader-pretty Southern belle.

Blythe recalled Cait mentioning that although Bobbie-Sue's family was well-off, determined to make it on her own, she was working as a waitress at Flynn's while waiting for her "big break."

She handed Lily and Blythe each a menu. "So," she said to Blythe, returning to her original topic, "did you manage to track down Natasha?"

"Finally."

"Did she have any details to tell you about Alexandra and Patrick?"

"She filled in a few blanks."

"Does that mean the project's still on?"

"Definitely." Blythe waited for the inevitable sales pitch and audition request.

"Well, I'm happy for you. Cait told me how important this project is to you." Bobbie-Sue's smile appeared absolutely genuine, making Blythe feel rather guilty when the girl left without lobbying for a part in the film.

"Bobbie-Sue is awfully nice," Lily said. "But you know, I get the impression she's a lot tougher than she looks."

"Aren't we all," Blythe murmured. "Have you ever seen her act?"

"No. But her credentials are certainly impressive." Connor told me she's played Laura, in *The Glass Menagerie* at Yale. And the Elizabeth Taylor role in *Suddenly Last Summer.*"

"I suppose Tennessee Williams makes sense," Blythe decided. "With that accent."

"I suppose so. But she also did a lot of Neil Simon during summer stock."

Blythe looked at her Lily with renewed interest. "Sounds as if you're taking up agenting in your spare time." Not that Lily could have all that many extra hours in her day, Blythe considered, what with a new baby, a new home, a wedding to plan and having gone into partnership with Gage.

Lily's grin was quick and as filled with life as it had once been. Before she'd married that adulterous, thieving rat, J. Carter Van Cortlandt. "Connor's agreed to test her. And Brenda, too," she said, naming Bobbie-Sue's best friend. "But not because I suggested it," she said quickly.

"Of course not," Blythe agreed, knowing that there was nothing Connor Mackay would not do for Lily.

"Really," Lily insisted.

"Speaking of Connor, when are you two going to get married?"

"I don't know." Lily sighed and dragged her hand through her long corn silk blond hair. "If it were just the two of us, I'd marry him tomorrow."

"Last time I checked the wedding vows, only two people were involved."

"True. But Connor's not just anybody."

"No. He's the man you love."

"The *rich* man I love," Lily stressed, strain etching a line across her smooth forehead.

"I thought you'd moved past having problems with Connor's money."

"I have. And, I'll even admit that after worrying about how I was even going to buy baby food, it's kind of nice knowing that I'm not going to run out of money at the end of the month."

"Not unless you decide to buy Trump Tower and the Taj Mahal in the same month," Blythe agreed. "So, if it's not the fact that your husband-to-be is a gazillionaire, what's the problem?"

"The problem is the wedding itself. I've already been through one three-ring circus of a ceremony. I was hoping, if I ever got married again, I could keep it simple. With just a few family and friends. But, now that I'm marrying Connor—"

"I can't see him not going along with anything you want," Blythe broke in. "Have you discussed this with him?"

"Of course."

"And?"

"And, he says I should have whatever wedding I want."

"I still don't get it. If you want a small, intimate ceremony, and Connor agrees that whatever you want is all right with him, then what's the big problem?"

"A small wedding was all right when I thought he was Mac Sullivan. But he isn't Mac. He's C. S. Mackay."

"Whatever his name, he's the same man you fell in love with, Lily." They'd been over this ground before, as well. When Lily had first discovered Connor's deception and broken things off. "The same man who loves you to distraction."

"I know." She sighed again. "But Connor is an important man. My God, Blythe, he was *Time's* Man of the Year when he was only twenty-five and they're always quoting him in the *Wall Street Journal.* He's famous, which means that we should probably have a wedding that lives up to his status."

Blythe stared at Lily. "I can't believe I'd ever hear you parroting Madeline Van Cortlandt's snobby words. You do realize, of course, that's the same argument your former mother-in-law used to make you give up your dream wedding when you married Junior?"

"I know." Lily's expression was bleak. "And Connor keeps telling me that he wants a marriage, not a merger, but—"

"Connor's a smart man. And a good man. My advice is to marry the guy quick, before he gets away."

"Connor would never leave." On this, Lily's belief was absolute.

Blythe smiled, pleased to see the return of Lily's confidence. "I know. It's been obvious from the start that he's the kind of man who sticks around, like in the vows, for better or worse, richer or poorer, sickness and health."

"Like Gage."

"Like Gage," Blythe agreed with a soft smile.

"So, perhaps we should start planning *your* wedding."

"Clever how you so deftly managed to change the focus," Blythe said dryly. The bar was suddenly flooded with bright California sunlight as the door opened. "There's Cait," Blythe said, relieved that the conversation would be forestalled.

Even dressed in the properly sedate navy suit she'd worn to testify at a trial this afternoon, Caitlin Carrigan still garnered the attention of every male in the bar. Heads turned, as if on swivels, as she crossed the bar on her long, purposeful stride.

"Welcome back," she said, exchanging a hug and kiss with her childhood friend.

"It's good to be home," Blythe said. "How did things go in court?"

"The entire case was thrown out of court because the coroner's office misplaced the damn lab results. So, thanks to a monumental bureaucratic screwup, the judge had no choice but to grant the defense's motion for a dismissal." Storm clouds billowed in her green eyes. "Which means, that in another hour or so, we're going to have another rapist walking the streets."

"I'm sorry," Blythe said.

"The hardest thing was explaining to the victim of date rape how the system let her down. Especially since it took me hours to talk her into prosecuting the bastard in the first place."

"What happens now?" Lily asked.

Cait cursed and rubbed her temples with her fingertips. The emerald engagement ring Sloan had given her flashed like green fire in the muted bar light. "I made a couple of calls and it looks as if the feds may take her case. Since the creep in question was her supervisor, we're hoping we can at least nail him on a sexual harassment charge."

"That's better than nothing," Blythe said encouragingly.

"That's what I keep telling myself," Cait agreed glumly. Struggling for the professional detachment that she'd always found the most difficult part of police work, she shook off her frustration, both mentally and physically.

"Changing the subject to yet another heinous crime, Sloan tells me you've got some good stuff on Alexandra's murder."

"I think so." Blythe had already decided to tell Lily and Cait about the dreams. She was hoping they'd be able to convince her of what Gage had not—that the nightmares were merely the project of an overactive imagination, stimulated by her obsession with Alexandra.

For the next ten minutes she shared what she'd learned about the problems in Alexandra and Patrick's marriage, including their argument the night of the New Year's Eve party. She also told them about having dreamed that Alexandra was pregnant.

"Did the autopsy reveal a pregnancy?" Cait asked.

"No. But that doesn't necessarily mean anything."

"Are you saying you think there may have been a cover-up?" This from Lily.

Blythe shrugged. "That's possible, I suppose. But conspiracies are hard to pull off because all it takes is one person talking and the entire thing unravels. Besides, in this town, secrets are harder to keep than marriage partners.

"It's probably more likely that since it was easy to determine that Alexandra had died by strangulation, that the coroner didn't delve any further."

"But that's what autopsies are supposed to do," Cait pointed out.

"True. But let's face it, the murder was more than sixty years ago and things were different. Even these days, with all the tools of modern science, mistakes can be made. As you've just pointed out."

"There *is* the possibility that you're mistaken," Lily suggested gently. "About Alexandra being pregnant."

"No." Blythe realized how strange the swift denial sounded, given the facts of the case. "I can't explain how I know, but I'm absolutely positive that she was carrying Patrick's child."

"This is going to sound crazy," Lily said tentatively. "But have you considered the fact that perhaps those dreams you've been having are Alexandra's spirit somehow talking to you? Trying through you to absolve her husband?"

"Believe me, Lily," Blythe said honestly, "three months ago, I would have laughed at the idea."

"And now?"

"And now, I'm not willing to discount any possibility. Including the fact that Alexandra Romanov is telling me that her husband was executed for a crime he did not commit."

"You know, this conversation just keeps getting more and more depressing," Cait said. "So, moving on to more pleasant topics, congratulations on moving in with Gage."

"How did you know I'd agreed to that? I only made the decision a few hours ago."

"I *am* a detective," Cait pointed out with a flash of her usual humor. "Actually, Gage told Lily, who called me at the courthouse."

"News certainly travels fast."

"Always does, in this town," Cait agreed. "I figure by this time next week exaggerated stories of your sexy

Grecian Island love nest will be scooped up by shoppers in checkout lines all over America."

"Unfortunately, you're probably right." Blythe said. "In fact, believe it or not, when we were waiting at the Athens airport, I saw our picture in *Tachidromos.*"

The candid photograph, which had earned the cover of Greece's leading national picture magazine, of Blythe and Gage dancing together had been taken during the wedding reception they'd attended. Anyone looking at the captured moment might have been excused in mistakenly thinking *they* were the happy couple.

The love she felt for Gage had been written all over her face—and in her eyes. Viewing it, Blythe understood why neither Lily nor Cait had believed her when she'd claimed she wasn't falling in love with the sexy private detective.

So, why couldn't she just agree to marry him? She needed time. Time to think.

The thought had no sooner flowed through her mind when Blythe remembered something Gage had said to her. He'd accused her of thinking too much. And, although she hated to admit it, this was one of those cases when he could be right.

Perhaps it was having grown up surrounded by adults who played make-believe for a living, perhaps it was her own way of finding logic in a business that revolved around fantasy, or perhaps, it was merely her nature, but for whatever reason, Blythe had always felt more comfortable when things made sense.

When they were safe. And predictable.

Unfortunately, love was anything but logical. And nothing about her feelings for Gage made any sense. Neither were they safe or predictable.

But she could no more stop from feeling them than she could stop the sun from sinking into the Pacific Ocean every evening. Or cause the tide to cease its age-old ebb and flow.

As hard as she'd tried to avoid it happening, the truth was that she'd fallen in love with a man who was as devoted as he was exciting. As trustworthy as he was dangerous. As honest as he was passionate.

She could take all the time in the world, she could try to analyze her feelings for Gage Remington from now until doomsday, but she'd never have the answers she was seeking. Or the guarantee she'd once thought she needed.

Love didn't come with guarantees.

Love didn't come without risk.

Now, as she vaguely listened to Cait and Lily discussing Cait's wedding plans, Blythe came to the unpalatable conclusion that her unwillingness to make a complete commitment to Gage was due to a deep-seated, private fear that having lost control of her heart, she was also in danger of losing control of her life.

The one thing she'd neglected to factor into the equation was that she'd fallen head over heels in love with the one man worth the risk.

10

THE SPORTSMAN'S SALOON definitely went overboard in trying to live up to its name. Mounted fish and hunting trophies—deer, elk, mountain lion, antelope, big-horned sheep—hung on knotty pine walls. A Kodiak bear stood in the corner, towering threateningly over whoever ended up with the last stool at the end of the L-shaped bar.

As he nursed a draft beer and listened to Michael Connelly's fishing plans, Gage couldn't quite shake the feeling that he was being silently observed—and judged—through all those unblinking marble eyes.

"You ever fish for steelhead?" the elderly man asked.

Michael Connelly was a large man, built like a rail-road boxcar, darkly tanned, with beefy arms the size of Virginia hams. He was wearing well-worn jeans, a flannel shirt and boots. The sleeves of the black-and-green plaid shirt had been rolled up to his elbows. His right forearm was adorned with a blue tattoo of an anchor; the right bore a red heart with the name *Ethel* inscribed across the center. Had he not known better, Gage might have taken the man for a former lumberjack who'd earned his living cutting down the towering ponderosa trees that surrounded the town.

"Can't say as I have," Gage said. "I've caught a few catfish in my time—"

"Trash fish," Connelly snorted dismissively. "But they're not bad deep-fried in a beer batter," he allowed.

"That's the way my Grandma Remington used to fix them back when I was a kid growing up in Whiskey River, Arizona," Gage agreed. "My dad preferred bass."

"Too damn expensive for my taste." The former detective tossed back his Jim Beam. Gage signaled the bartender for a refill. "Had a friend who near went broke, by the time he finished paying for his boat and all that fancy, newfangled electronic sonar equipment. Guy had more stuff on board than we used to search out Nazi U-boats back when I was on submarine duty during the war."

He rubbed his chin, home to a grizzled pewter beard. "Don't remember it helping him find all that many fish. Old Jack never was much of a fisherman. But he could sure tell crackerjack stories about the one who got away."

"Speaking of ones who got away," Gage began carefully.

Michael Connelly slammed his glass down onto the nicked pine bar. "Thought I told you, young fella, digging around in graveyards is a good way to end up causing a helluva stink."

"Or clear the air," Gage countered.

The man's answer was a pungent curse spat out through teeth yellowed from years of tobacco. "Dead's dead. No amount of second-guessing is going to change that."

"You're right. But what about the murderer? What if he's sitting in some bar tonight, planning to go fishing tomorrow?" Gage shook his head and took a drink of beer. "Doesn't seem fair, somehow."

"You'd think you would've caught on, having been a cop and all," Connelly said. "Sometimes—hell, most of the time—life isn't fair."

"You've got a point," Gage conceded again. "Still, sometimes I just get the urge to go tilting at windmills." When his assertion drew a blank look in return, he said, "You know, like Don Quixote."

Connelly shook his head. His baseball cap, which appeared to have once been white, but was now the color of mud, was a billboard for Big Al's Bait Shop.

"Never much liked that artsy stuff they made us read in school. Give me Zane Grey and Jack London any old day."

"How about Dashiell Hammett or Raymond Chandler?" Gage eyed the former L.A. detective over the rim of the pilsner glass. "You like reading them?"

Michael Connelly may have been in his eighties. But his blue eyes were bright and direct. He speared Gage with a stern, accusatory glare.

"You don't give up easy, do you, boy?"

"No, sir." Gage's look was every bit as direct. "I don't."

There was a long silence as Connelly mulled that over. He pulled a cigarette from a pocket of his shirt, broke off the filter tip, then stuck it between his grimly set lips. Another foray into the pocket retrieved an old-fashioned kitchen match which he struck on the sole of his boot.

Gage wondered if the slight hand tremor, as he lit the cigarette, was due to age or discomfort in talking about a case the former cop would prefer to forget.

Utilizing his customary patience, Gage waited.

"You gotta understand how it was," Connelly said finally. "The world we were all working in." He drew in on the cigarette. "These days, everything is fair game — a married actor screws his leading lady on some beach he thinks is deserted, two days later the photos are plastered across the front page of a supermarket tabloid.

"Or a teenage sitcom star throws a tantrum and throws a punch at her boyfriend in an after-hours club, and bingo, that night Leno and Letterman will be making jokes about it in their monologue."

He pursed his lips, blew a perfect smoke ring and watched with satisfaction as it slowly wafted upward toward the ceiling. When the blue circle settled over an antler, Gage decided it was a trick the old man had spent a long time perfecting.

"Back in the old days, a helluva lot more happened in the movie community than was made public. Like the Fatty Arbuckle case. And the Paul Bern suicide." He shook his head. "It's no wonder that poor loser shot himself in the head with that .38. Imagine being married to Jean Harlow and not being able to get it up."

Connelly blew another smoke ring. "It'd be like not getting an erection while watching a Blythe Fielding video."

Irritation flared, white-hot inside Gage. Figuring he'd have to get used to the idea that men all over the world fantasized about bedding the woman he loved, he managed, with effort, to tamp it town.

He also suddenly understood how difficult it must have been for Reardon, knowing every male who'd ever stepped inside a theater was lusting after his wife. For not the first time since discovering the truth about the actress's less than pristine past, he found himself wondering if Reardon *had* known about Alexandra's former occupation.

"You were telling me about the Romanov murder," he coaxed the elderly man back on track. "About the difference between people's perception of Hollywood and the truth."

"People talk about the good old days. When the studios existed just to make movies. Hell, from the beginning, they looked out for their own interests before anything else. That's what the publicity departments were established to do—to see that the scandals never got out."

"But some scandals are too big to cover up." Gage knew the press was always hungry for scandal. And Alexandra Romanov's murder by her husband had provided a virtual feast that had lasted long after Reardon's execution.

"That's true," Connelly allowed. "And whenever those scandals did get out, the flack machine kicked into high gear, pumping out propaganda, twisting whatever facts were necessary to make the ticket-buying public believe whatever the studios wanted them to believe."

He took out the rumpled pack of cigarettes again, broke off another filter and lit the shortened cigarette from the smoldering end of the first.

"Of course no one gave a damn what truths they might be obscuring. Or even whose lives they might be ruining. The important thing was that the studios, and the guys that ran them, came out smelling like roses."

"Is that what happened in the Romanov murder? Was the truth obscured?"

"Obscured?" The laugh turned into a hacking nicotine cough that went on and on. "Hell," he managed finally, "try buried. Six feet deep. Right along with Reardon's ashes."

"The press only prints what it's given," Gage said. "I understand how Xanadu Studios may have wanted to slant things to its own advantage, but there must have been reporters on the L.A. papers with sources inside police departments. And surely there must have been some frustrated cops willing to leak facts to those reporters."

When Connelly didn't answer, Gage realized he may be looking at something that went a lot deeper and got a lot darker than murder.

"If the police department, for whatever reason, aligned itself with the studio bosses, you'd be talking about the hindrance of a criminal investigation on a major scale."

Broad shoulders lifted in shrug. "I couldn't argue with that."

"Following that line of thought," Gage suggested slowly, carefully, "it's also possible that the Los Angeles Police Department—"

"Don't forget the D.A.'s office," Connelly broke in.

During his teens, Gage had owned a German shorthair dog named Flick. Right now, he figured he knew exactly how Flick had felt pointing out a covey of quail.

"You realize, if Reardon didn't do it, you're talking about the entire legal system being guilty of aiding a criminal—a murderer—to escape."

"I'm not talking about anything. You're the one headed off down that trail, boy." The vague, purposefully evasive answer proved that police training never wore off.

Gage was beginning to get the feeling that the trail in question was no longer going to turn out to be a dead end.

"You were the first detective on the scene, weren't you?"

Connelly nodded. "Me and my partner, Hank Greene." He eyed Gage's empty glass. "You want another?"

Seeing that the former cop's glass was empty again, Gage ordered another round. "Tell me what you found."

Another shrug. "There wasn't all that much to find. The murder took place in a dressing room that was part of the master bedroom suite. The lady was lying on the floor, in front of this huge ugly mother of a mirror, deader than Marley's ghost. From the bruises on her throat, it didn't take a medical genius to see that she'd been strangled.

"There were two glasses and an open bottle of champagne on a table. One of the glasses had lipstick on the rim, the same color worn by the victim. The other looked untouched. A cigarette had been stubbed out in a crystal ashtray on that same table. Since there weren't any lipstick traces on it, we figured it was probably Reardon's."

"What was she wearing?"

"It was more like what she wasn't wearing." A long smoldering flame of lust sparked in the former detective's eye. "It was one of those negligee things, white and lacy, trimmed in some kinda fancy white feathers and so transparent a blind man could probably read the fine print of a used car contract through it.

"You should have seen Hank." He laughed, coughed, then cut the cough off with a swallow of whiskey. "The guy was still a kid, just outta school and I'm not sure he'd ever seen a naked woman before. One look at Alexandra Romanov definitely put the wind in his sails. So to speak."

"I've seen the pictures," Gage said without a trace of an answering humor. He'd never found anything the slightest bit funny about homicide.

"Most people have." Connelly flashed a lascivious grin. "I heard later that the police photographer retired to a ranch outside Mt. Shasta with the dough he got from selling those bootleg pictures to the papers."

One of the more depressing aspects of a homicide scene was the way the victim lost any sense of dignity. It was bad enough having a cabal of cops looking at you after you'd lost the ability to protect yourself; having the world gain access to the intimate photographs taken at a crime scene added an additional note of vulgarity to an already unsavory situation.

"You didn't find any sign of a struggle?"

"Nah. That, along with the see-through nightie and the champagne glasses pointed to the fact that the lady was intimate with her murderer."

"That's the case the prosecutor made in court," Gage agreed. "But there are several other possibilities. One being that the killer could have broken into the house and taken her by surprise while she was waiting for her husband to come home."

"That'd be a little difficult. Since Reardon admitted the door was locked when he came home and supposedly found her body."

"Someone else could have had a key."

"From the rumors about her, there's a good chance half the guys in town had keys to Alexandra Romanov's house."

"Rumors?" Gage lifted a brow. "What kind of rumors?"

As if realizing he'd said too much, the cop stared down into his glass, as if seeking a hiding place in the smooth brown depths. "You know," he mumbled, "wild parties, drinking, the typical Hollywood stuff. The fact that she wasn't really a member of the Russian royal family."

Michael Connelly knew a lot more than he was telling. Gage would bet his P. I. license on it. "A lot of people arrive in Hollywood pretending to be someone they're not. If lying about your background was a capital crime, the only stars we'd have left would probably be Mickey and Minnie Mouse. And who really knows about Minnie? I mean, where, exactly did she come from before she started up with the Mick, anyway?"

"Anyone ever tell you that you're warped, Remington?"

"All the time. Which is why I'm in private practice these days." Gage paused, then drove the arrow he'd been saving home. "So, how about Cuba?"

"What about it?" Connelly's tone, and his look, turned suddenly defensive.

"I would assume someone did a background check on Alexandra."

"Probably."

"I would also assume that it wouldn't have been all that difficult to learn how she'd made a living in Havana."

"Seems to me she was some kind of model."

"Among other things."

Connelly didn't answer. His stony expression revealed nothing, but from the red flush rising from the man's plaid flannel collar, Gage knew he'd hit the bull's-eye.

"Mind if I theorize?" he asked.

"Don't see that I have much to say about it."

"Good point. Anyway, it would seem to me," Gage said mildly, "hypothetically speaking, of course, that if the police discovered that Xanadu's major star had once worked as a prostitute, in a wide-open gambling town literally run by the mob, that might open up a few avenues of investigation."

"It might. Of course, there's always the chance, *hypothetically speaking*, that more than one of those avenues might lead straight to the husband."

"Granted." It was, Gage admitted silently, something he had been forced to consider himself. "But, if that was the case, you'd think the D.A. would have brought it up at the trial. To show motive."

"Wasn't any need. All the nails were already in Reardon's coffin from the beginning."

"So there was no point in endangering Xanadu Studios' golden reputation."

Connelly lit another cigarette. His stare was a hard cold one Gage had used himself on more than one occasion. "Interesting theory you've got there."

"I think so." No slouch in the intimidation department, Gage stared back. "I also think that it could have been *your* theory. Before you were pulled off the case."

"I wasn't pulled off. I quit."

"Oh, yeah, I almost forgot that part." Gage nodded. "Let's see, the way I heard it, you were the department's golden-haired boy, the most likely to make lieutenant before you were thirty. Hell, you probably could have ended up a division commander. Or chief."

His smile held not a trace of humor. "Makes sense to me that you'd trade all that upwardly mobile success to move to a faraway town where the biggest crime to investigate would be overturned outhouses and the occasional rustled steer."

Connelly didn't even attempt to answer the unspoken accusation. There was no need. "Alexandra Romanov was killed more than sixty years ago. Why the hell are you dredging things up now?"

Gage shrugged. "Better late than never."

Connelly's answer was a muttered curse.

"Mind if I try a little more theorizing?"

The old man spread his beefy arms in a be-my-guest gesture.

"I think that you realized the case was taking on a life of its own," Gage said. "I also think you weren't real wild about the way it was going. You thought Reardon was a little too pat. Too obvious."

"Crimes of passion happen."

"True. So do crimes for profit."

"You saying you think she was professionally hit?" Disbelief radiated in the roughened tone.

"No. But you've already said that times were different. That the studios held a massive amount of power and influence. Let's say that stories about Alexandra's past were beginning to surface. Or, perhaps, for one reason or another, she was considering leaving Xanadu, which would result in a drastically diminished cash flow.

"The country was in the grips of the Great Depression. Only two studios—Xanadu and MGM—were operating in the black. If Alexandra walked, or her career was ruined because of scandal, all the big shots in the executives at Xanadu—including Walter Stern—might have started jumping out of windows."

"The problem with that theory," Connelly argued, "is you've just pointed out why no one from the studio would have killed her. Because a dead actress can't bring people into the theater."

"Now that's where you're wrong," Gage said. "You know as well as I do that there's nothing the esteemed members of the press—and the people—love more than a scandal. In fact, by the time Xanadu premiered *Fool's Gold*, releasing it the week Reardon went on trial, the film broke records in every city all over the country.

"Alexandra's last role, written by her husband, made so much money, Stern got the bright idea to release all her old films. Xanadu was the first studio ever to do that, and the other owners thought he was nuts. But the box office receipts allowed him to ride out the rest of the depression in style."

"You're accusing Stern of making money off Alexandra's murder. But isn't that exactly what Blythe Fielding's doing?"

"Blythe's motivation is different."

"Sure." There was another short, hacking laugh. "The lady thinks she's going to play Nancy Drew and solve a crime. And, she may just get lucky and come close. But in my business—and in the one you used to be in—coming close doesn't cut it.

"In a movie, it's enough if you get the facts kinda right. Once the story gets up on that big screen, it'll be taken as the truth. And hell, it just may be the truth. But my job was solving murders. Which means I didn't have the luxury of speculation. I had to make damn sure I got the facts of the case exactly right."

"Or the wrong man could die," Gage said quietly.

Connelly didn't answer. Instead he turned and stared out the window at the lake beyond the asphalt parking lot. It had begun to rain; water streamed down the dingy glass, hammered on the tin roof.

"Look, you gotta understand. In those days, L.A. was a wide-open town. We had booze flowing like the Niagara, dope, prostitution, gambling. Our job was supposedly to clean things up, but most days I felt like the guy in a circus parade, following after the elephants with a teaspoon.

"The only way to survive the system was to follow orders. If my lieutenant told me to jump, I'd ask, 'How high?' If he told me to look the other way when some sergeant I was riding with stopped and picked up an envelope from a bookmaking joint, I put on blinders. If I was told to raid one speakeasy and ignore the one right next door, that's exactly what I did."

"And if that same lieutenant told you to ignore crucial evidence in a murder investigation—"

"I'd say *No way, José.*" The granite jaw thrust out. From the steady, implacable look in Connelly's eyes, Gage knew he was telling the truth.

It didn't really matter whether or not Connelly had been pulled off the case, then quit, or if he'd quit knowing he was going to be replaced. The truth, as unpalatable as it may be, was that in the Alexandra Romanov case, truth and justice had gotten ground up by the heavy wheels of corruption.

"How high up did it go?" Gage asked quietly.

Connelly looked away again. "Did it ever dawn on you that some people might not like the idea of you and that Fielding broad looking into a closed case?"

"You said it yourself. The murder was more than sixty years ago."

"True." Connelly turned back and gave Gage a long look of warning. "But I'm still kicking. So, what makes you think I'm the only one left from those days?"

Good question. "I don't suppose you'd be willing to name names?"

"Not on a bet." He rubbed his stubbled chin. "But, if you don't have anything else to do, you might run an address check on Paul Young."

"The former Los Angeles County D.A.?"

"Got it on the first try." The mirthless yellow grin was back. "He quit right after Reardon was executed. Last I heard, he'd moved to Barbados. And he wasn't exactly camped out on the beach, if you know what I mean."

His wink spoke volumes. Gage tossed some bills on the bar to pay for the drinks and held out another.

"Put your damn money away," Connelly growled. "There's no need to pay because I didn't tell you a damn thing." His eyes narrowed again beneath the brim of his mud brown cap. "Understand?"

Gage nodded. "Absolutely." He stood up, prepared to leave. "Have a good fishing trip."

"If it's half as successful as yours has been, I'll be satisfied," the former homicide detective said dryly.

As he walked out into the rain, headed toward his rental car, Gage knew that Blythe had been right all along. Patrick Reardon had been railroaded.

Two thoughts crossed his mind simultaneously. The first being Connelly's warning about people still being alive that wouldn't want the truth about the case to get out.

The second thought was, if Reardon didn't kill Alexandra, perhaps the makeup lady was right. Perhaps Walter Stern *had* killed Xanadu's biggest star.

ALTHOUGH SHE WAS looking forward to living with Gage, Blythe wasn't entirely comfortable with the idea of moving into his apartment without him being there. Though he'd given her a key, she decided to spend one more night in her hotel. Then, after Gage returned from Oregon, she'd make the move.

It seemed a logical plan. Until Alan Sturgess showed up at the door of her bungalow while she was packing the rest of her things.

"We need to talk," he said without preamble.

"There's nothing to talk about," she insisted. A well-placed foot kept her from closing the door.

"We left things badly." Deftly moving past her, he entered her living room. When he saw the suitcases, more than she would have needed for her brief trip to Greece, he arched a brow. "Going somewhere?"

"Not that it's any of your business, but I'm moving into an apartment."

"I told you you'd get tired of living in a hotel."

His smugness, which she'd once taught herself to accept, grated. "So you did."

"You know," he said, softening his tone and his expression, "there really isn't any need for you to move into some tacky, impersonal apartment." He ran his hands up her arms. "I've plenty of room at my house."

"Are you asking me to move in with you?"

"Of course. We did, you recall, discuss it before."

"And I'm sure *you'll* recall that you were afraid that cohabiting with a woman who wasn't your wife might hurt your chances for being named chief of staff." His stroking touch gave her the willies. Blythe backed away.

The only hint of his irritation was a faint narrowing of his eyes. "I'll admit to perhaps being overly cautious. But don't forget, after the earthquake, *I* was the one who suggested you move into my home." His practiced smile was warm, coaxing feminine compliance. Blythe wondered if it was the same one he used to convince a potential patient to have a nose job and some silicone cheek implants added to a planned face-lift. "The offer still stands."

"Wouldn't it get a little crowded?" she couldn't resist asking. "With you, me and Brittany all living under the same roof?"

"Brittany was an aberration," he said, dismissing the actress with a negligent wave of his well-manicured hand. "The entire affair started out because she was so terrified of surgery. I will admit, that my efforts to soothe her fears may have gotten a bit out of hand."

"A bit?" Blythe dragged her hand through her hair and stared at this man she'd once been engaged to, as if seeing him for the very first time. "Alan, even discounting the fact that you were unfaithful to me, you were sleeping with a patient. Excuse me if I don't recall sexual healing being part of the Hippocratic Oath."

"I wasn't the first doctor to fall victim to the lure of a predatory patient. I doubt if I'll be last."

Blythe was not surprised that he was trying to blame this on Brittany. Disappointed, but not surprised.

"Predatory *and* needy," she mused, not bothering to keep the sarcasm from her tone. "I suppose that's an irresistible combination for any man."

Accustomed to her formerly accommodating behavior, Alan seemed both surprised and annoyed by her refusal to cave in as he'd obviously believed she should. "I didn't come here to rehash old arguments."

Blythe crossed her arms. "Why did you come here?"

"To convince you there's no need to break off our engagement just because of a slight lapse on my part."

It was a lot more than a lapse, but Blythe knew there was no point in arguing. Alan had always viewed things through the filter of his own perceptions. If he didn't believe something was important, then it wasn't. His constant dismissal of her work, especially her Alexandra project, had only been one example of his egocentric mind-set.

"You may have a point," she allowed.

"That's my girl." Self-satisfaction was written all over his handsome face.

When he moved toward her again, Blythe backed away. "There are probably cases where infidelity, while not overlooked or forgotten, could at least be forgiven. Unfortunately, Alan, this isn't one of them."

"What the hell does that mean?"

She sighed, suddenly feeling very tired. "It means that there are other reasons I can't marry you. Reasons that have nothing to do with Brittany. Or any other women you may have slept with while we were engaged."

"I believe I'm entitled to know those reasons."

Actually, he wasn't. But Blythe decided to tell him anyway. "I don't love you, Alan."

Heaven help her, she'd tried. Really she had. But with the twenty-twenty vision of hindsight, Blythe realized that she'd been holding something back from the beginning. Which is why she hadn't been devastated when she'd discovered him in the pool with Brittany. Having invested nothing emotionally in their relationship, she couldn't be hurt.

Unlike Alexandra. Whose love for Patrick had been all-consuming.

"I told you, Blythe, I never expected a marriage based on love. Love makes a lousy foundation. It never lasts."

"That's where you're wrong, Alan," Blythe argued calmly, once again thinking of Alexandra and Patrick. Their absolute love for one another, she knew, was never-ending.

"What's reason number two?" he asked, as if realizing that he wasn't making any grounds chipping away at the first one.

"I'm in love with another man. A man I intend to marry." The moment Blythe heard herself say the words, she knew it was what she wanted. "As soon as possible."

"I don't believe it." He stared at her, nonplussed. "When did this happen? *How* did this happen?"

"I've had feelings for Gage for several months, but I suppose you could say I was in denial. As for how it happened—" Blythe shrugged "—the usual way."

"You can't possibly be referring to that detective you hired?" He heaped an extra helping of scorn on Gage's occupation. "Remington, wasn't it?"

"That's his name. And yes, that's who I'm talking about."

Storm clouds gathered in his blue eyes. "You slept with the guy in Greece, didn't you?"

"That's none of your business."

His lips curved into a faint, knowing smile. "It won't last, you know. You're too different."

"About some things, yes. But not in all the ways that matter."

The realization that nothing worth having, even love—especially love—was without risk had come to her over the past months as she'd worked on her project.

Only a few days ago, Blythe had been trying to convince herself that marrying Gage would be impossible. Now she knew that the impossibility would be *not* marrying him.

"I can't believe you're doing this."

"And I'm sorry you can't understand," Blythe said honestly.

A muscle jerked along his jaw. "Not as sorry as you're going to be," he predicted. "Married to some struggling, ex-cop who spends his days peeping into motel room windows."

"Gage is a good man. And a great detective. I'm proud of him. And I'm especially proud of the way he's chosen to spend his life helping people."

He shook his head, looking at her as if seeing her for the first time. "I thought I knew you. It's discomfiting to realize I was wrong."

"Don't feel like the Lone Ranger," Blythe advised him easily as she looped her arm through his and began walking him to the door. "Because I'd always thought I knew myself. And believe me, Alan, it's come as a major shock to realize that *I* was wrong."

Despite the seriousness of the conversation, Blythe couldn't keep the smile from blooming on her face as she thought about where she would be going when she left here.

He was about to leave when he turned in the open doorway. "I can't guarantee I'll be waiting when you finally come to your senses."

"I didn't expect that you would be."

Blythe watched her former fiancé leave and realized that a chapter in her life was ending. But she felt not a twinge of regret. Because a new, exciting, wonderful one was beginning.

Ten minutes later, she was driving down Sunset Boulevard, headed toward Bachelor Arms.

11

WHENEVER BLYTHE VISITED Bachelor Arms, she experienced a strange feeling of déjà vu. Tonight was no different. As she walked past the plaque, where some unseen hand had scratched *Believe the legend*, she felt goose bumps rising on her arms.

"Someone walking across my grave," she said, murmuring the old wives' tale. The thought, along with the building pewter clouds overhead and the electrically tinged scent of an impending storm did nothing to calm her feeling of discomfort.

Telling herself that she was letting her encounter with Alan get to her, she concentrated on thinking positive thoughts. Like welcoming Gage home tomorrow night with a candlelit dinner. Naturally, they'd begin with champagne. And oysters on the half shell, not that Gage needed any assistance in the virility department.

A steamed salmon fillet with white wine and caper sauce might be a nice entrée, she mused, then instantly reconsidered. Gage was definitely a meat and potatoes man if she'd ever met one. A grilled steak, she decided. With roast potatoes and a Caesar salad. With such a heavy dinner, she'd forego a rich desert, choosing instead some ripe berries.

They could eat them later, in bed. With more champagne. After making love.

On second thought, she reconsidered, remembering those passionate, love-filled hours they'd spent in their

lovely alcove bed on Aegina, the entire dinner could
wait.

She was smiling, humming tunelessly as she walked
across the courtyard of Bachelor Arms when she realized someone was following her. All too aware of the
lateness of the hour, she spun around, holding her key
ring out in front of her like a weapon.

"Walter?" She stared in disbelief at the man she'd mistaken for a mugger.

"Hello, Blythe." His smile was the same insincere flash
of capped teeth she was accustomed to seeing, but there
was stress in his eyes. "Nice evening, isn't it?"

What was he doing here? Surely he hadn't dropped by
to discuss the weather? And how did he even know to
find her here at Bachelor Arms, anyway?

"Actually, it looks as if we're in for a thunderstorm."

"Really?" Seeming surprised by that, he glanced up at
the threatening sky. "Why, you're right. It is getting a bit
overcast."

Having never been overly fond of Walter Stern when
she was forced to do business with him, Blythe was not
particularly anxious to spend time chatting with him
now.

"What are you doing here, Walter?"

Irritation flared; Blythe watched him struggle to tamp
it back down. "I need to talk with you."

"Is it really that important? I've had a very long day,
and—"

"This won't take long. And yes, it's more than important. In fact, you could say it's vital. To both our fu-
tures."

Well, she couldn't deny that he'd gotten her attention
with that one. "All right," she said with an uncharacter-

istic lack of graciousness. "Come on in. But I'd appreciate it if you could keep it short. I really am exhausted."

"I shouldn't wonder," he agreed, with another one of those smiles that didn't reach his eyes. "Even a workaholic like you must succumb to a twinge of jet lag."

Since his tone wasn't the faintest bit complimentary, Blythe didn't answer. Neither one spoke until they'd reached Gage's apartment.

"How did you find me, anyway?"

"I passed you as you were leaving the Chateau Marmont and I was arriving."

"Are you saying you actually followed me here?"

"I suppose you could say that. But it wasn't as if I were stalking you, Blythe. I just needed to speak with you. Alone."

She gave him a long look, then decided she had nothing to be concerned about. Until recently, Walter Stern had been one of the most powerful men in town. And although he might temporarily be out of a job, knowing that he was not the kind of man to stay down for long, she doubted he'd do anything to risk his reputation.

Of course there was that time Cait had busted him during a prostitution sting, Blythe considered. But, if all the stories regarding a famous Hollywood madam were true, he certainly wasn't the only wealthy, powerful man in Hollywood willing to pay for sex.

"All right," she said reluctantly. "You may as well come in."

"I said alone. What I have to discuss with you can't be said in front of that detective you've hired."

"Gage isn't here."

"He isn't?"

"No." Deciding there was no point in keeping Gage's mission a secret, she said, "Here's in Oregon tracking down a lead on the investigating detective who was first at the scene."

He didn't respond to that remark as she'd expected. "So he gives you the key while he's gone?"

"Actually, I'm moving in." She lifted the overnight case she was carrying.

Surprise moved across his still handsome face. "That must have been some successful trip to Greece."

"It was enjoyable," she responded as she passed through the entrance to the hallway and approached the apartment door.

"And informative?"

"Actually, it was. Natasha Kuryan proved quite helpful."

"I told you she's a liar."

"So you did. You also told me she was crazy." Blythe unlocked the door. "But although she's admittedly a bit eccentric, she certainly seemed rational to me."

"I assume you've heard about what happened at the studio," he said, abruptly changing the subject.

Obviously, Blythe considered, this was the reason he'd tracked her down tonight. She hoped he wasn't going to ask her to plead for his job back.

"About your decision to retire?"

"We both know I didn't leave willingly, Blythe. I was forced out. By your new friend."

"I didn't have anything to do with that, Walter," she said calmly as she went around the living room, turning on lights. In the distance, thunder rumbled ominously.

"But you weren't surprised."

"No." There was nothing to be gained by lying. "I'll have to admit that when I first learned Connor was the man who'd purchased Xanadu, I couldn't picture the two of you working very well together."

"You've never liked me, have you?"

She could be equally direct. "Not really. For some strange reason, I've always found the idea of a grown man pawing a young girl offensive."

"That's not the signals you were giving off at the time."

"For heaven's sake, Walter," Blythe flared, "I was fifteen years old. Even if I'd known how to give off signals, which I didn't, you should have kept your damn hands off me!"

A muscle jerked along his jaw; a vein pulsed at his temple. "That's what this is all about, isn't it?" he said in a low, threatening tone that reminded her of a hungry timber wolf. "You're using your friend's lover to get back at me after all these years."

As angry and tired as she was, Blythe couldn't help laughing at that. "That, more than anything proves my point about you and Connor not being able to work together.

"If you had the faintest idea what made Connor Mackay tick, you would realize that he would never— under any circumstances—misuse his wealth and power. The idea that he'd force you out of the studio that has been in your family for three generations as some personal vendetta for me, is ludicrous."

"That's what you say."

The air thickened as the walls seemed to crowd in on her. Blythe blamed the strange sensation on the storm. "It's the truth."

They were at an impasse. Silence settled over them. Disbelief was written all over his handsome face as he glanced dismissively around the room. His gaze stopped on the mirror. "That's the ugliest damn thing I've ever seen."

Momentarily distracted, Blythe felt an odd compulsion to defend the overly ornate mirror, even though it always made her a little uneasy. "It happens to be a very valuable antique."

"I don't care if it was owned by Marie freaking Antoinette. It's still ugly as sin."

Blythe didn't want to talk about the mirror. Actually, she didn't want to talk to Walter Stern about anything. She just wanted him gone. Out of the apartment and out of her life.

"Well, now that I've assured you I'm not behind any conspiracy to get you out of Xanadu, I think it's time for you to leave, Walter."

"I suppose you've also sweet-talked Mackay into backing your latest project," he said, ignoring her request.

"I didn't have to sweet-talk anyone into anything. My contract with Xanadu allows my production company to make one film of my choice for every two films I star in for the studio. I believe the definitive words are *my choice.*"

"But Mackay's behind the film."

"Yes. He thinks it has Oscar potential."

Walter Stern's answer to that was somewhere between a curse and a laugh. "That just goes to show how much the guy knows about the business. The Academy won't vote for a film that doesn't have mass audience appeal. And trust me, sweetheart, your little melodrama will die on opening weekend.

"People go to the movies for adventure, to watch things get blown up. They don't lay out money in order to waste two hours watching the rehash of some ancient murder of a actress everyone's forgotten by a one-book hack writer."

"Actually, Patrick wrote several books. But the others were pulp westerns written under various pseudonyms."

"I suppose that's something else your detective discovered."

"No." Blythe paused for a moment, a bit puzzled by her knowledge herself. "I must have read it somewhere."

"Whatever, the movie's going to be another *Heaven's Gate.* Or *Ishtar.*"

"You're welcome to your opinion." She left unstated the reality that his opinion no longer mattered. At least not at Xanadu Studios.

"You'll be sorry," he warned in a low, threatening tone she'd never heard from him before. "You'll all be sorry."

Unwilling to dignify the threat, Blythe was about to insist he leave, when the phone rang.

Thinking the call might be from Gage, she made a dash for the desk across the room. "Hello? Oh, hi, Lily. No, you weren't disturbing a thing." She glanced back over her shoulder. "Don't let me keep you, Walter."

She heard the door open and shut as she chatted with Lily. Yes, she'd moved out of the hotel and no, she hadn't heard from Gage as she'd hoped.

When she hung up after the brief conversation, Blythe was relieved that Walter had, indeed, gone.

Her mind drifted, as it so often seemed to these days, to Gage. As she crossed the room to lock the door, Blythe caught sight of her reflection in the mirror. The unconscious smile reflected in the glass was definitely that of a woman in love.

Was this how Alexandra had felt about Patrick? she wondered. Had her thoughts constantly turned to him, even when she was supposed to be thinking about her work?

"Yes." Blythe's smile widened. "Yes, this is exactly how Alexandra felt." As an actress, she was grateful for the insight. As a woman, for not the first time since she began researching the glamorous star, Blythe felt a definite kinship.

Intending to retrieve the rest of her belongings from her car, Blythe was almost out the door when she caught a glimpse of something out of the corner of her eye. She spun around.

"I don't believe it," she murmured, staring at the shimmering image in the mirror. The ebony-haired woman, dressed in a long pale gown, was standing very still, gazing unblinkingly out at Blythe. "I know Cait and Connor both were supposed to have seen you. But to tell you the truth, I didn't really believe you existed."

As a crack of thunder rocked the apartment, Blythe tried to tell herself that the woman was merely a product of an overly active imagination, exhaustion, and jet lag.

But she knew, deep in her heart, that the image was all too real.

The room brightened in the glow of a phosphorescent lightning flash. "According to the Bachelor Arms legend, my favorite wish is supposed to be granted. Or my greatest fear realized."

That possibility sent a frisson of fear skimming up her spine. Gage was scheduled to return home tomorrow. What if his plane crashed? What if she lost him? Blythe resolutely blocked off that unpalatable thought. "So, which is it?"

The woman in the mirror did not respond. But her slow, odd smile seemed to be an answer in itself. There was another burst of thunder and right on top of it, a flash of lightning.

The lights flickered, then went off, throwing the apartment into darkness.

GAGE HAD NEARLY reached his motel when he slammed on his brakes, nearly throwing the car into a skid on the wet road. After correcting, he made a U-turn, headed back to The Sportsman's Saloon.

Fortunately, Connelly was right where he'd left him, perched on the wooden stool, engaged in a fly versus bait argument with the bartender.

"Forget something?" he asked when looked up and saw Gage standing beside him.

"That cigarette in the ashtray," he said, "what made you think it belonged to Reardon?"

"It was in Alexandra's bedroom. If it wasn't his, then the lady was obviously entertaining intimate visitors."

"Reardon didn't smoke."

Connelly looked at Gage with reluctant interest. "How the hell do you know that?"

It was a question Gage couldn't answer. "I just know," he said doggedly.

The former cop shrugged. "Doesn't mean anything. In fact, if he came home and found evidence of some other man boinking his wife, it makes sense he'd be more likely to kill her."

"I thought you didn't believe Reardon committed the murder."

Another shrug. Connelly took a long drink of his beer, then wiped the foam off his mouth with the back of his hand. "Got a point there."

"Another thing. That mirror in the dressing room. Can you remember what, exactly, it looked like?"

"I'm not likely to forget it," Connelly said with a grimace. "It was huge—four feet by five, probably. It was made out of some kinda metal—you know, that heavy silver stuff?"

"Pewter?"

"That's it." He nodded. "It was also ugly as sin, with all sorts of scrolls and rosebuds all over it."

Apprehension rose. Thunder rumbled ominously in Gage's head. "Do you happen to remember where, exactly, this house was?" he asked with a calm he was a very long way from feeling.

"Sure." Gage was forced to tamp down impatience as Connelly polished off the beer. "It was in the Wilshire district." The address he rattled off from memory turned out to be the same as the one for Bachelor Arms.

"That can't be right." But somehow he knew it was. "The records show the murder scene to be three blocks away." Gage and Blythe had both visited the scene, discouraged to find it had been razed during the 1960s in order to build a strip center minimall.

"The records are wrong." Connelly lit yet another cigarette. "The first person to call the crime scene in was a cop who'd had his cruiser pulled over by the Reardon's hysterical housekeeper. The cop got pretty flustered as well and called in the wrong address to headquarters. The papers picked it up from the initial police report, and since no one ever thought to change it, that's what it stayed."

"How the hell could the wrong address get into the trial records?"

"Things happen."

Especially in a situation where no one with ties to Xanadu—including undoubtedly Patrick's defense attorney—were interested in determining the truth.

"Besides," Connelly said with a shrug, "the mistake worked out well for the cops because it kept all the lookey-loos away from the crime scene."

Not that there was any real investigating going on, Gage thought furiously.

"What about the other house? Surely the people who lived there complained about all the sudden attention?"

"It was vacant. It belonged to a producer who'd lost his shirt in the stock market and ended up taking a triple gainer off the top of the Hollywood sign. The place had gone into foreclosure six weeks before the murder."

"But surely there were people who knew where Alexandra and Patrick lived," Gage pressed on doggedly.

"Not that many. They'd just moved from her place that Christmas."

Gage decided that explained why Natasha hadn't mentioned anything about living in Alexandra's former home. Obviously the former makeup artist had no idea her apartment was located at the scene of Hollywood's most infamous murder.

And Blythe ... She was moving in tonight. Into the very room where Alexandra had been strangled. Gage's blood turned to ice.

12

THE PRIEST WAS YOUNG, with a thin pale face and the sorrowful eyes of a depressed bloodhound. "It won't be long now," he said for the umpteenth time that night.

In no mood for conversation, Patrick didn't answer.

Although his mission was to soothe the prisoner's last hours, it was obvious that the priest, fresh out of the seminary, didn't have the faintest idea where to begin.

"Would you like to pray?" he asked.

Patrick shook his head.

"How about something to eat?" the young man tried again. "You didn't touch your dinner. You must be hungry."

Although there was absolutely nothing humorous about his situation, Patrick almost laughed at the suggestion. "That's a little irrelevant, right now, wouldn't you say?"

A dark pink rose from the stiff white collar. "I'm sorry." Long slender fingers combed through carrot red hair. "I'm afraid I'm not doing a very good job of this."

Patrick sighed, taking pity on the young man who was so obviously in over his head. "You're doing fine, Father."

"Really?" A spark of hope appeared in those bleak eyes.

"Absolutely." Patrick figured, since he was about to

be executed for murder, a lie wouldn't mean much in the general scheme of things.

"They say it won't take long."

The priest's musical brogue conjured up scenes of emerald green fields, thatch-roofed stone houses and rugged rocky coastlines. Gage thought about the trip he and Alexandra had planned to the land from which his grandparents had emigrated.

They'd been scheduled to sail the day after the premiere of *Fool's Gold*. And although Alexandra, accustomed to sunshine and warmth from her years in Cuba and Los Angeles, had fretted about taking the trip in winter, he'd promised to do his husbandly duty and keep her from getting chilled. A promise they both knew he was more than capable of keeping.

After four weeks touring the country, including visits to relatives in his ancestral counties of Antrim and Wexford, they'd return to the States, and to his ranch in Wyoming, where they—along with the half-dozen children Alexandra insisted she wanted—would live happily ever after.

That had been the plan. Unfortunately, experience had taught Patrick that the best laid plans usually went astray.

"You know, my son," the young man, who was a decade younger than Patrick, offered hesitantly, "it's my duty to advise you to make a good Act of Contrition. So God will absolve you of your sins before..."

"I'll be meeting my Maker soon enough, Father," Patrick cut him off mildly. "I can't see how one prayer's going to make that much of a difference when compared to a lifetime of misdeeds."

"The church teaches absolution for our sins. Surely you wouldn't be thinking of turning your back on a sacrament?"

"I appreciate the offer." Gage's tone was polite but firm. "But I think I'll take my chances."

Seeds of worry appeared in eyes the crystal blue of a Kilkenny lake. "'Tis a dangerous madness you're talking."

"Haven't you noticed, Father? The entire world's gone mad. One more lunatic probably isn't going to make much of a difference. In heaven or in hell."

"The bishop isn't going to like this," the priest complained, more to himself than to Gage.

"Don't worry, Father." Gage surprised the priest with a wink. "I won't tell him if you don't."

Blue eyes observed Gage gravely. "It's a very strange man, you are, Mr. Patrick Reardon."

"So I've been told." The most recent person to call him crazy had been his own attorney, when he'd refused to take the stand in his own defense.

"But an innocent man, I'm thinking," the priest concluded.

Patrick managed a grim smile at that, thinking that this was the first person, including his lawyer, who believed that.

No, he recalled, there'd been another. That detective who'd been the first on the scene. Conlin? Coughlin? Connelly. That was it. Unfortunately, Detective Connelly, wherever he'd disappeared to, had ended up becoming yet another victim of a corrupt system.

"Didn't anyone ever tell you, Father?" Patrick's smile was a grim, humorless slash. "Death Row is filled with innocent men." To Patrick's knowledge, not one of his fellow inmates had admitted to the crime he was to die for.

The priest was forestalled from answering by the arrival of the prison guard. "It's time," he announced in a low voice that was reminiscent of the funeral toll of a church bell.

Patrick pushed himself up from the wooden table in the cramped visitor's room. Although he was admittedly not looking forward to the next few minutes, anticipation flowed warmly in his veins.

Because, from that first moment he'd seen Alexandra Romanov, Patrick had recognized the tempestuous Russian actress to be his destiny. That being the case, he had not a single doubt that he was about to be reunited with the only woman he'd ever loved. The only woman he could ever love.

For all eternity.

GAGE WAS FORCIBLY and rudely jerked awake. Struggling his way out of the netherworld of nightmares, he dragged a hand down his face and was surprised to find that sweat was pouring down it.

"We've just run into a little bad weather," a feminine voice soothed. "It's nothing to be alarmed about, Mr. Remington." The flight attendant, who'd begun hovering over him when he'd first boarded the plane, smiled reassuringly. "Would you like a warm towel?"

"Thanks."

He took the white towel with hands that were not nearly as steady as he would have liked. It was not that he was afraid of flying. It was the nightmare that had him drenched in sweat. A nightmare he knew, as impossible as it would sound to most people, as it would have

sounded to him only a few days ago, had not been a
dream at all, but a long buried memory.

Although it made no rational sense, Gage knew that
Patrick Reardon was innocent.

And the reason he knew that with such rock solid certainty was because he'd once lived in Patrick Reardon's
skin.

On top of that incredible thought came another. One
even more frightening than the memory of his own
death.

The woman he'd fallen in love with—again!—was in
danger.

Nerves humming, Gage retrieved the phone from the
armrest, ran his credit card through the slot and dialed
the number of his apartment. Surely by now Blythe
would have settled in.

Frustration surged through him when a recorded voice
told him that all the circuits were busy, to please try his
call again. Gage looked down at his watch. There were
still thirty minutes until the plane landed at LAX. Thirty
minutes that loomed like an eternity.

IT WAS RAINING, a torrential downpour that made Blythe
decide to retrieve the rest of her suitcases from her car in
the morning.

Although she didn't relish the idea of getting soaked
by the drenching rain, Blythe wasn't particularly disturbed by the Pacific storm raging overhead. Indeed, as
she slipped beneath Gage's crisp navy sheets and
breathed in his scent on the pillow beneath her head, she
felt immediately soothed.

With thoughts of the man she loved in her mind, she
drifted off into a deep and dreamless sleep.

ALTHOUGH GAGE HAD SPENT countless hours on stake-outs, he'd never known time to move so slowly. As the jet made its descent into Los Angles, visions kept flashing in his mind, one after the other, like those flipping calendar pages marking the progression of time in old black-and-white movies. Movies like *Lady Reckless*. And *Fool's Gold*.

He remembered their fight the night of the New Year's Eve party. Furious by rumors of her infidelity, not to mention the revelation that the wife he adored had been a high-class prostitute, he'd lost his temper and said cruel, hurtful things he hadn't really meant.

He had no idea how many hours he'd walked along the Santa Monica beach. But by the time he was ready to return home, he knew that he would have to apologize for having judged her too harshly.

Now that he'd calmed down, he accepted that what she'd done to survive was in the past. He also knew that the stories of her having committed adultery were lies. Alexandra could no more cheat on him than he could on her. They were each other's destiny. They were soul mates. Now that they'd found each other, nothing—or no one—could come between them.

THE MAN, dressed all in black, crept past the front door of Bachelor Arms, keeping to the shadows. He paused as he passed the words scratched below the name plaque.

"Believe the legend," he read aloud. His soft laugh was thick with menace. Hollywood lived on legends. And, he considered darkly, occasionally died on them, as well.

He made his way to the apartment without encountering anyone. Which wasn't surprising, considering the storm. Residents of Los Angeles were accustomed to warm sunny weather; a little rain and they behaved as if they might melt, like Margaret Hamilton's Wicked Witch of the West in *The Wizard of Oz*.

It grated on his nerves that the film had won an Oscar after Xanadu had turned the project down, calling it nothing but an overwrought remake of the old silent film.

The door to the apartment was, unsurprisingly, locked. But he'd expected that and had come prepared. He inserted the slender metal wire into the lock. With a deft twist of the wrist, it gave way.

The apartment was dark. He flicked on a small penlight and made his way to one of the the the bedrooms.

Blythe was dreaming of Gage. They were back in Greece, alone in a secluded cove. They were swimming nude, side by side, in water so clear and so warm it seemed like another world.

Drifting naturally into his arms, Blythe gave herself up to the pleasure of his lips, of the feel of his strong body pressed against hers.

The dream shifted to one of Alexandra and Patrick together at his ranch in Wyoming, lying in front of a fire.

Outside a blizzard was raging; inside there was sizzling warmth, generated more by his clever, wicked touch than the dancing orange-and-red flames.

"You're my woman." His voice was as rough as the gray stones of the fireplace.

His hands, as they bruised over her flesh, created sizzling trails of heat. His lips sparked fierce, untamed desires.

"Yes." Wild to touch him, as he was touching her, needing to possess him as he'd possessed her, she clutched at his shoulders as she took him deep inside her. "And you're my husband. My lover. My everything." The words, spoken in her native language, needed no translation.

Their eyes met. Visions blurred as they began to move to the unrelenting rhythm of their shared need. Passion poured out of him into her; love flowed out of her into him.

"Forever," they said in unison, as they soared, joined for all time, into the flames.

THE BEDROOM WAS LIT with the stuttering glow of lightning. The man in black stood beside the bed, watching her toss and turn on the mattress, listening to her murmured sighs and soft moans. When she cried out a name, an iron fist clenched his heart. His gut. And lower.

He'd always known what she was. He'd understood that she'd been born to tempt men, and until she'd given her heart away to another—a man who could do nothing for her!—he hadn't minded. It was, after all, the price a man must pay for possessing a goddess.

But now she'd betrayed him. And for that, she must pay.

The hand moved up her cheek, rousing her from the erotic dream. At first Blythe thought that it was Gage. But as she arched against the caress, like a cat wanting to be petted, she realized that there was something wrong.

The fingers on her face were encased in leather. She drew in a sharp breath and recognized the familiar scent of expensive cologne.

"Alan?"

"Shh." He covered her mouth with a gloved hand. "Don't scream. And don't call for help." He touched the tip of the razor sharp scalpel to her throat. "Do you understand?"

A flash of lightening illuminated a face that was at the same time both familiar and unrecognizable. Madness glowed in the eyes of this man she'd thought she'd known. A man she'd tried so hard to love. Terror, as cold as ice, as sharp as the blade of the scalpel, crawled beneath her flesh.

Forbidden to speak, but afraid that moving would result in a life-threatening wound, Blythe managed the faintest of nods.

"Good girl." Alan Sturgess flashed a grim, humorless smile. A muscle jerked beside his thin lips. "Now, I want you to get out of that bed very slowly. And then I want you to come with me."

This had to be another nightmare, Blythe assured herself. It couldn't really be happening. Soon she would wake up and the sun would be shining and Gage would be home and she would tell him about her decision to marry him—as soon as possible—and then they'd spend the rest of the day and night making slow, wonderful love.

"I said, get the hell out of that bed."

When she felt the blade prick her skin, Blythe knew this was no idle threat. Folding back the sheets, she gingerly left the bed, grateful for the darkness that kept him from being able to see her body through the translucent white silk nightgown.

"That's better." He took hold of her arm. "Now, come with me."

"Where are we going?"

Her question was answered with a swift, painful backhand to the side of her face that had her head reel-

ing. "I told you not to say a word." This time he pressed
the flat edge of the scalpel against her cheek. "Next time,
I'll use this. Then we'll see how much work you can get."
His voice was soft, but strained. "How many fans would
want to see a scarred, disfigured Alexandra Romanov,
do you think?"

Blythe's first thought, as he took her arm and pulled
her into the living room, was that in whatever madness
had taken over Alan's mind, he'd confused her with the
murdered actress.

But then there was another rumble of thunder that
rattled the windows and a flare of lightning that lit up the
sky and the room like the blinding glow of Fourth of July
fireworks.

When Blythe saw their reflections in the pewter mirror, she finally understood everything. The man standing behind her, the man with the scalpel pressed against
her throat outwardly resembled Alan Sturgess. But behind the madness in his eyes, she viewed the terrifying
truth.

The panic bubbled up. For a moment she thought it
would overwhelm her. Closing her mind to the terror, she
concentrated on extricating herself from this potentially
fatal situation.

"It was you, wasn't it?" she managed in a remarkably
reasonable voice, considering the circumstances. "You
killed Alexandra, didn't you, Walter?"

"This is all your fault," he insisted. "*I'm* the one who
found you. *I'm* the one who made a star out of a casino
hotel hooker. I made you everything you are. Gave you
more than you ever dreamed. But it wasn't enough." She
felt the prick of the blade against her icy skin, felt a trickle
of warm blood.

"Walter—"

"Shut up!" His voice was no longer soft or controlled. The strain had been replaced by a ragged emotional tremor. "Or I won't be responsible for the consequences!"

His fingers curved painfully around her upper arm again as he dragged her out of the apartment. Blythe considered screaming for help, then, knowing all too well his unparalleled skill with a blade, decided she had no choice but to go along with him for now. When she realized where he was taking her, she knew that escape was going to be difficult, if not impossible.

He was literally dragging her up the stairs to the turret that rose above the apartment house. When her foot caught in the hem of the nightgown, she fell to her knees.

"Get up!" Now he was screaming, the madness in his voice equaling that in his eyes. He jerked her to her feet and began dragging her up those steep narrow stairs again.

Her heart was beating wildly in her throat. She'd never realized that it was possible to be ice-cold and sweating all at the same time. The door to the turret opened on a creak of rusty hinges. As he pushed her inside the room, Blythe almost fell again.

"You don't want to do this," she said, stalling for time as her fevered brain tried to figure a way out of this nightmare. "Not really." Although it took every vestige of her acting ability, she managed to force her voice into a calm, yet sultry tone, the tone of a woman cajoling an angry man to reason. "Not after all we've been through together, Walter."

A possessive man, Walter Stern, founder of Xanadu studios, had treated Alexandra like the rest of his expensive playthings. In all ways, until she'd met Patrick, Alexandra had allowed Stern to become her absolute lord.

He watched her like an eagle watched his prey, supervising her scripts, approving every morsel of food that passed between her ruby lips; he chose her clothing, her hairstyles, her cars, her house and her friends.

A cruel man with the inborn instincts of a tyrant, Walter patronized her, taunted her and often humiliated her. But he'd also taken a nobody, and with the mysterious, infinite gift of a creator, had breathed life into her nothingness, fulfilling his promise to make her a star.

"That's my point, exactly." His voice turned soft again in a way she found even more terrifying than his out-of-control shout. "I made you, Alexandra Romanov." He ran the blade down her throat, across her shoulders, the swell of her breasts. "And I'm going to be the one to destroy you."

The scalpel gleamed deadly in the lightning flashing all around them. With a single, swift slash of the blade, he ripped the white nightgown from neckline to hem.

Gage drove like a maniac on the way from LAX to Bachelor Arms, breaking speed limits and running red lights. As he pulled up in front of the building with a screech of brakes, the total absence of lights told him that the storm had knocked out the power. He grabbed the 9 mm pistol from the glove compartment and dove out of the car. As he ran up the sidewalk, a crack of lightning illuminated the building in a ghostly white glow.

For some reason, his gaze was drawn to the turret. What he saw through the floor-to-ceiling windows made his pounding heart clench.

She was not going to die, Blythe assured herself. Not this time. Not just as she'd reclaimed the love that had been so cruelly taken from her.

Once before she'd tried to reason with this man, once before she'd been arrogant enough to believe that her bountiful arsenal of feminine wiles could prove more powerful than madness. Unfortunately, in the end, she'd failed. And both she and Patrick had paid a fatal price for her feminine arrogance.

This time she would fight. Not just for her own life, but for the life she and Gage would have together.

Fate proved to be on her side as the sound of brakes squealing, followed by a car door slamming outside, distracted Walter/Alan's attention. Fear, fury, hatred, all echoed in her shout as she suddenly shoved against him with every ounce of strength she possessed. He stumbled, the scalpel clattering to the wooden floor. Both of them dove for it at the same time.

Gage heard her scream. He couldn't be too late! Not again. He took the stairs two at a time, cursing viciously when he found the door locked. Furious enough to rip it off the hinges with his bare hands, he instead shoved his shoulder against the wood, splintering the jamb.

He found the man he knew to be Walter Stern standing in the center of the room, a scalpel in his right hand. She was backed up against the wall, her eyes wide, her chest heaving. When he saw that her nightgown had been torn down the front, he thought of all the evil this man had done. And how he would gladly kill him for hurting her.

"It's over," he said. "You're not going to get away with it. Not this time." Gage gestured with the pistol. "Put the scalpel down. Nice and slow."

The killer's only answer was a vicious curse. Then he charged like a mad bull, the deadly blade aimed directly at Gage's heart.

Instincts honed during years of police training allowed Gage to deftly step aside, avoiding the thrust. There was the sound of glass shattering. Then a high-pitched scream, followed by the heavy thud of a body hitting the stone courtyard.

And then there was only the soft, gentle sound of rain falling on the roof as the violent storm passed on.

Epilogue

THE DAY OF THE WEDDING began as yet another California day in paradise. The scent from brightly colored, blossom-laden bushes filled the warm air with their sweet perfume.

In the courtyard of Bachelor Arms, a three-piece string ensemble was entertaining the small gathering of family and guests seated on rented white satin-seated chairs. All the residents of the apartment building were on hand for the triple wedding.

Natasha Kuryan, home from Greece, was in the front row, seated between Blythe's parents and Connor's mother, who was dangling a set of keys in front of her fascinated granddaughter. Delicate pink rosebuds bloomed on Katie's ruffled dress; the elastic band circling her head was adorned with a matching, tiny pink silk rosebud. The baby gurgled happily as she reached for the shiny keys with her pudgy baby hands.

The three grooms, waiting beneath a trellis of sweetly fragrant wisteria, were, of course, uniformly handsome in black tie.

When the musicians broke into the wedding march, the assembled guests all turned to view the brides. They were all beautiful, as brides are supposed to be on their wedding day. Cait's flamboyant, fiery coloring, Lily's deceptively fragile pale blondness, and Blythe's sultry dark gypsy looks, provided attractive foils for one another.

Cait looked even more stunning than usual in a full-skirted silk gown with a sheer illusion back that rustled enticingly with each step. Her green eyes were clear, her stride long and self-assured. The only sign of nerves was the splash of bright color on her high cheekbones.

Following her, a beatific Lily walked in beauty up the white satin runner, her long, strapless white organza gown topped by a sheer, silk chiffon jacket. She was carrying a simple nosegay of sweet peas. The guests breathed a soft sigh, in unison, as she paused and pressed a brief kiss atop her baby's blond head.

For her aborted wedding to Alan Sturgess, Blythe had chosen a simple, sophisticated dress that had caused Cait to complain at the time that a wedding gown should be more romantic.

Today's dress definitely fit that criteria. The off-the-shoulder fantasy gown was a froth of white lace and seed pearls, fit for a fairy-tale princess.

One look at Gage's uncharacteristically stunned expression assured Blythe she'd chosen well.

As she reached his side, Blythe smiled up at this man with whom she'd already shared so much. Together, they'd cleared the name of an innocent man. And solved a sixty-year-old murder. Like all detectives, Michael Connelly had kept a notebook of his investigation. That notebook, which had arrived by courier without any accompanying letter, provided Sloan with the ending for his screenplay. The accusation that Walter Stern had murdered his biggest star would, Blythe knew, hit Hollywood like a bombshell.

As for Alan, the police had written the physician's seemingly aberrant behavior as yet another tragic case of a murderous lover scorned. Only Blythe and Gage knew the truth.

The words were simple. Complex. And timeless.

As she shared a look more eloquent than words with this man she loved, Blythe knew they'd spoken these vows before. But today, as she repeated them, her voice ringing out strong and sure, she felt as if she were saying them for the very first time.

To love. Honor. Cherish.

For better or worse. Richer or poorer.

Forsaking all others.

Till death do us part.

Without taking his eyes from hers, Gage slipped the woven gold band onto her finger. Her hand, far steadier than her heart, then placed a gleaming symbol of promise on his finger. Having exchanged rings, they now exchanged smiles.

As Gage bent his head, Blythe knew that the vows had it wrong. A love as strong as theirs could never be constrained by mere physical limitations like life and death. Having been cruelly denied the lifetime together they'd pledged to one another so many years ago, they'd miraculously been given a second chance.

Their lips touched, their first kiss as husband and wife.

Then, as the musicians played and her mother wept, and the rest of the guests enthusiastically applauded the trio of newlyweds, Gage and Blythe turned and walked, hand in hand, down the white satin runner toward their future.

Temptation

THREE GROOMS:

Case, Carter and Mike

TWO WORDS:

"We Don't!"

*ONE
MINI-SERIES:*

GROOMS ON THE RUN

Starting in March 1996,
Mills & Boon Temptation
brings you this exciting new
mini-series.

Each book (and there'll be one a
month for three months) features a sexy
hero who's ready to say "I do!" but ends up
saying, "I don't!"

Look out for these special Temptations:

In March, I WON'T! by Gina Wilkins
In April, JILT TRIP by Heather MacAllister
In May, NOT THIS GUY! by Glenda Sanders

MILLS & BOON

This month's
irresistible novels from

Temptation

STRANGER IN MY ARMS by Madeline Harper

Secret Fantasies

Do you have a secret fantasy? Kasey Halliday does. She's
always wanted to be swept off her feet by a dark, handsome
stranger. Will Eastman, Kasey's enigmatic new neighbour, fits
the bill perfectly. But when mysterious accidents start to occur,
Kasey realizes more than just her heart is in danger...

THE TEXAN by Janice Kaiser

The 500th Temptation

Brady Coleman vowed to bring his sister's killer to justice. But
the rough-and-tumble Texan desperately needed the help of
beautiful Jane Stewart. And when her vulnerable heart longed for
Brady, how could she refuse?

JILT TRIP by Heather MacAllister

Grooms on the Run

Carter Belden was *not* having a good day. He was supposed to be
getting married, but his best man was late, his pager wouldn't
stop bleeping and then he was kidnapped before the ceremony—
by his ex-wife!

THREE GROOMS AND A WEDDING by JoAnn Ross

Bachelor Arms

Ever since Blythe Fielding had hired private investigator Gage
Remington to solve a decades-old mystery, she had had second
thoughts about walking down the aisle with her fiancé. Gage was
sexy, dangerous and compelling. How could Blythe resist the
unknown passion his eyes promised her?

Spoil yourself next month
with these four novels from

Temptation

THE LAST HERO by Alyssa Dean

Rebels & Rogues

For Commander Wade Brillings, duty came first. So when he
suspected that beautiful Cassandra Lloyd was part of a
smuggling ring, he had to stick close to her. *Really close.*
Experience told Wade to keep his hands off her, but his heart
said something else…

THE TEMPTING by Lisa Harris

Secret Fantasies

Do you have a secret fantasy? Carol Glendower does. She wants
her husband back—alive and well. A mysterious turn of events
means Carol now has a chance to find Evan again. Are her
dreams taunting her? Or is there a chance that this could be for
real?

NOT THIS GUY! by Glenda Sanders

Grooms on the Run

Single-mum Angelina Winters couldn't believe her luck when
she met charming Mike Calder. For a while, she thought she and
Mike had a good thing going, but then she saw his list of what he
wanted in a woman and realized she scored a perfect zero!

LOVERS AND STRANGERS by Candace Schuler

Bachelor Arms

Cynical reporter Jack Shannon hoped that by moving back to
Bachelor Arms, he could lay old ghosts to rest. Sexy Faith
McCray had a few ghosts of her own. She wanted to give Jack all
the love he'd ever need—but was he brave enough to accept it?

Temptation

Coming up in
BACHELOR ARMS...

When Blythe Fielding planned her wedding and asked her two best friends, Caitlin and Lily, to be bridesmaids, none of them had a clue a new romance was around the corner for each of them—even the bride!

These entertaining, dramatic stories of friendship, mystery and love by **JoAnn Ross** continue to follow the exploits of the residents of Bachelor Arms. If you loved the male Bachelor Arms titles you'll love the next set coming up in Temptation featuring the female residents of this lively apartment block.

Look out for:

FOR RICHER OR POORER (March 1996)
THREE GROOMS AND A WEDDING (April 1996)

Available from WH Smith, John Menzies, Volume One, Forbuoys, Martins, Woolworths, Tesco, Asda, Safeway and other paperback stockists.

Temptation

Do You Have A Secret Fantasy?

Everybody does.

Maybe it's to be rich and famous or to have a no-strings affair with a sexy mysterious stranger. Or to have a sizzling second chance with a former sweetheart...

You'll find these dreams—and much more—in Temptation's exciting new year-long series, Secret Fantasies!

Look out for **The Tempting** by **Lisa Harris** in May 1996.

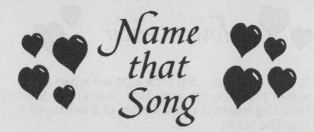

Name that Song

How would you like to win a year's supply of simply irresistible romances? Well, you can and they're free! Simply solve the puzzle below and send your completed entry to us by 31st October 1996. The first five correct entries picked after the closing date will each win a years supply of Temptation novels (four books every month—worth over £100).

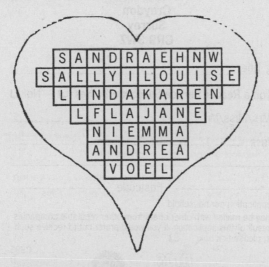

	S	A	N	D	R	A	E	H	N	W
S	A	L	L	Y	I	L	O	U	I	S	E
	L	I	N	D	A	K	A	R	E	N
		L	F	L	A	J	A	N	E
			N	I	E	M	M	A
			A	N	D	R	E	A
				V	O	E	L

Please turn over for details of how to enter ☞

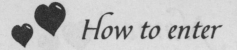 *How to enter*

To solve our puzzle...first circle eight well known girls names hidden in the grid. Then unscramble the remaining letters to reveal the title of a well-known song (five words).

When you have written the song title in the space provided below, don't forget to fill in your name and address, pop this page into an envelope (you don't need a stamp) and post it today! Hurry—competition ends 31st October 1996.

Mills & Boon Song Puzzle
FREEPOST
Croydon
Surrey
CR9 3WZ

Song Title: _____

Are you a Reader Service Subscriber?   Yes ❏   No ❏

Ms/Mrs/Miss/Mr _____

Address _____

_____

_____ Postcode _____

One application per household.

You may be mailed with other offers from other reputable companies as a result of this application. If you would prefer not to receive such offers, please tick box.   ❏

C396
D

mps MAILING PREFERENCE SERVICE   DMA